Ryker

The Powers That Be

Book 4

Harper Bentley

D1715260

Dedication

To anyone who's ever

had their heart broken

Hang in there, lovely

You never know what's

just around the corner!

1—Dual Meet

"I'm a whore."

Silence.

"I'm a big, humongous slut," I groaned into my phone.

Finally an answer. "No, you're not," my best friend Sharee Leppart assured with a sleepy chuckle.

"I am," I said with conviction. "I'm also a skank."

"Frankie, it's not that big a deal."

"I'm a total hussy. A floozy. An absolute bimbo. A *whore!*" I dropped my head against the steering wheel and closed my eyes.

"Look, practically everyone's had a one-night stand."

"Not me," I whispered. I heard her sigh before I added, "And not with the man of their dreams and all the while thinking it was special."

God. What the hell had I been thinking? God!

I'd waited two years for him. *Two years.*

And it finally happened.

I'd finally had him.

And it had been everything I thought it'd be and more.

He'd kissed me like I'd never been kissed before.

Then he'd made love to me as if I'd been the most precious thing he'd ever held in his arms.

He'd lain next to me afterward still holding me as we drifted off, his lips at my temple giving me sweet kisses.

We'd awakened a few hours later and he'd fucked me. Hard.

It was hot.

It was dirty.

He'd given me so many orgasms I lost count.

And I loved it, every last minute of it.

It was everything I knew it'd be.

And I'd been completely and utterly happy.

Afterward my bubble had burst.

"Thanks, darlin'. That was great. Gonna get a beer then I've gotta get some sleep. Leave your number on the fridge. I'll give you a call."

No temple kiss.

No squeeze of his arms.

Nothing.

I'd been dismissed.

Just… like… that.

He'd gotten out of bed and I'd stared at him in all his naked glory. When he'd turned his back to me to pull a pair of boxer briefs from his dresser, I'd found myself gaping at the tattoo emblazoned across his back, the one I'd always wanted to get a closer look at. And what I'd seen was a very scary grinning Grim Reaper. I'd studied the art for a moment seeing that there were two dead gladiators lying at the Reaper's feet, their faces skeletons like the Reaper's (yeesh), and he was battling yet another warrior whose face was just as scary and skeletal and intense as his.

I'd looked away and swallowed roughly, my throat hurting as I tried to keep the tears from coming. After he'd left, I'd gotten out of bed, dressed and slunk my way the hell out of his room, out of his house and into my car, not wanting to be noticed by anyone and *not* leaving my number.

Now I was in my car at five-thirty a.m. talking to Sharee.

"Where are you?" she asked.

"Parked on the street in front of his house after having just taken the walk of shame."

She snorted. "It wasn't a walk of shame. It was a walk of awesome, Frankie! You finally nailed Ryker Powers! You've wanted him forever!"

I sat back staring out at the rainy almost-dawn watching the rain sliding in rivulets down my windshield.

She just didn't understand.

I choked on a sob. "Ree, you don't get it. That's the father of my future children probably lying asleep in there right now after having fucked my brains out all night long! We're supposed to get married, have three children—two boys and a girl, the boys older than the girl so they can protect their sister of course—and then we're gonna grow old together!" My voice caught but I kept going. "And I've screwed it all up by jumping the gun! We were supposed to have a meet cute like in the old movies! Like, run into each other at a coffee shop and both grab for the sugar at the same time. After that we'd trade numbers and flirt for, like, a week. I'd lure him in with my womanly wiles and fabulous personality until he knew I was *the one*! After, we'd go on lots of amazing dates until he finally proposed at the top of the Great Wheel and I'd scream, 'Yes!' so loudly everyone on the ground would hear me and congratulate us when we get off it!" I sucked in several breaths before whispering, "Oh, my God.

What have I done?" I dropped my head into my hand knowing I'd messed up royally.

"Come home, Frankie."

She sounded a little put out which I'm sure she was. She was a realist. I was a dreamer. That's why we were best friends, opposites attracting and all that. But I guess I'd pushed her too far this time.

My head came up and I wiped away the tears that were the result of a dream lost. "All right," I mumbled as I put my Camry in drive. "You want me to pick up pastries?" I sniffed.

"Definitely."

Pulling away from the cute little house where inside my dream future had died, I wiped away a few more tears that had somehow slipped by without my notice and drove off into the gray and dreary morning.

~*~*~*~

After stopping by The Breakfast Nook to pick up the best pastries in all of Seattle, I headed back to Sharee and my apartment that was near Hallervan's campus, the college I'd be starting second semester tomorrow. It was my last semester since I was set to graduate in May with a degree in secondary English education with a minor in PE.

Last night's party had been sort of a last hurrah for me before I got really serious about my career. When Ciara and Madison, friends from the basketball team, had called yesterday afternoon telling me I was going with them, that I had no choice and they'd be by at eight, I'd thought, what the hell. Sharee had had to go to her older sister's wedding and I would've spent the evening alone, so I'd made myself up and followed the girls to the party.

Once there, I'd had a blast, getting to hang out with friends I hadn't seen in some time. And it was when I'd been in the backyard watching Ci and Mad own a couple football players at beer pong that I'd seen Ryker staring at me intensely from the patio and my breath had caught. He'd smiled at my wide-eyed look and headed my way. No, prowled was more like it, his long, powerful legs eating up the space between us like it'd been nothing, and, dear God, it'd been a sight to see.

When he made it to me, he'd told me I was the most beautiful girl there, which had made me all melty inside that he'd think that (the alcohol hadn't helped me see a pickup line when it'd been thrown right in my face). We'd talked for a bit about his wrestling and when he'd asked if I wanted to go somewhere quiet to talk, I'd jumped at the chance. Of course, we'd ended up in his room and all talking had ceased since our mouths had been perpetually fused from the moment we entered it, and I'd been thrilled, knowing my perfect future had been about to begin.

Now as I pulled into the complex, I sighed knowing I'd screwed with fate last night. From the way he'd treated me just now, I knew that Ryker had probably thought I was a Ring Rat, girls that hung around wrestlers just wanting to sleep with them (and since there'd been tons of them at his party, why wouldn't he?), and not someone he'd consider to be his future wife.

And that hurt.

"Hello, Francesca!" Mrs. Bertolini hollered from her patio which was above Sharee and my apartment. She came out every morning at seven in the dusty brown robe that had been her husband's, to have her cup of coffee and smoke two Pall Malls before starting her day as the director of arts and crafts at the senior center downtown. She herself was eighty-two but still as spry as a spring chicken in all her five-foot-two, ninety-pound glory, and I guess she kept those seniors on their toes because I'd seen some of their artwork displayed at various restaurants in Seattle and even around campus. She'd been a fairly good artist and sculptor in her day, had even taught classes at UDub, but arthritis had gotten to her hands so she'd had to stop. She'd lived above us the three years we'd been there, having moved in after her husband had passed, and was as sweet as can be. She didn't meddle but she did have an uncanny knack of knowing exactly what was going on with us. It was sometimes spooky how much she seemed to know, so much so that Sharee and I started thinking maybe she'd had a camera installed in our apartment and that's where she got her information. But her advice was usually spot-on (whether we decided to take it or not) which still wasn't any less eerie.

"Hi, Mrs. Bertolini," I said forcing a smile and giving her a small wave.

She narrowed her always-alert electric blue eyes at me sensing something was wrong. "Bad night?"

I shrugged as I shaded my eyes as I looked up at her. "Actually, great night. Bad morning."

She nodded like she understood which was ridiculous. "Aha."

"I've got some Breakfast Nook pastries. Would you like me to bring you any?" I called up.

"No, dear. You and Sharee enjoy."

"All right. See you later," I said as I started walking toward the hallway where my apartment and the elevator she used were.

"Gotta play it smart if you want his eyes to open," I heard her holler after me and I stopped for a beat before resuming my trek.

"She's eighty-two. How could she know?" I mumbled to myself with a frown thinking she was either psychic or just plain nuts. I decided I'd go with the latter for today and went inside to console myself with a few sugary pastries.

~*~*~*~

"So, you gonna do it?" Sharee asked that night after we'd had dinner and were now watching some shitty reality TV show.

I glanced at her from where I lay on the couch. "Why should I?"

She threw her legs over the side of the chair and a half she was sitting in to face me. "Because he needs to know. And for your children's future."

I gave her a pointed look. "He probably won't remember me."

She rolled her eyes. "Frankie. It was just this morning. He so will."

I looked at the TV for a moment before cutting my eyes back to her. "What am I supposed to do? Show up there and be like, 'Oh, hey, Ryker. I'm the chick you fucked all night long Saturday. Remember? So... wanna go out with me?'"

"Yes! Exactly that! Go to his house tomorrow morning before class and talk to him. Invite him to coffee or something. He'll see what a wonderful woman you are and fall madly in love with you. Then you can do the whole marriage, kids, future shit." She threw a hand out flippantly and scrunched up her face as she looked back at the idiot family on TV fawning over the pregnant daughter as if she was the first woman in the history of mankind to ever carry a child. But that wasn't why my roomie had gotten that look. No, it was that she'd just gone through a bad breakup and was a little down on love right now, so her giving me advice wasn't her favorite thing to do right now, which made me appreciate more that she had.

"All right. I'll do it. But if I get embarrassed in any way, you're so taking me for drinks at O'Leary's tomorrow night after my class."

"Done," she mumbled, her focus back on the TV.

I turned back also but my mind was on the next morning wondering if I should really go through with it. Oh, well, what could it hurt if I went by Ryker's house? All he could say was no and my future with him would remain as bleak as it was now.

No big deal.

2—Takedown

The next morning I was kind of a mess. I'd gotten up at six and since my first class wasn't until ten I showered and shaved my legs… twice (shaved not showered). I exfoliated my entire body and after drying off, slathered my face in a mask. While it dried, I plucked my eyebrows and checked to see if I'd developed a mustache between last night and this morning. Hey, I was Italian. It was entirely possible. I next checked my legs for any hair I'd missed. There were no stragglers, so I next peeled, rinsed, dried and curled, dressed and made myself up. Thank goodness I'd beaten Sharee in Rock-Paper-Scissors and won the master bedroom with the en suite so I hadn't wakened her with my raucous regimen. I took one last look in the mirror and was ready to go.

I went to Sharee's room and knocked lightly on her door. She was pre-law and didn't have a class until tonight and even though I was risking her wrath at waking her up, I needed some assurance.

"Pssst," I summoned when I opened her door.

"What," she muttered into her pillow that she had her arms wrapped around as she lay on her stomach.

"I just wanted to tell you I'm leaving. Wish me luck."

"Luck." She shifted and pulled the pillow over her head. I chuckled because I knew that was my cue to leave since she was definitely not a morning person. As I closed the door, I heard her add, "Love you. It'll be fine. Don't worry."

Sharee and I had been best friends since our sophomore year in high school. People often asked if we were sisters since we both had long brown hair and dark brown eyes, and of course we always said we were because we were goofy that way. But I'd grown up in Texas and when my dad had been transferred to Seattle with the oil company he worked for, she and I had become fast friends since we both played basketball and ran track. She was nearly six feet tall and had excelled at both sports and I hadn't done too poorly either. But where she'd played post in basketball and ran hurdles in track, I'd been a forward and had run the hundred meters since I was shorter. We'd made All-State in both sports and had been offered scholarships to play basketball at Hallervan where we were both All-Americans our first year. It'd been awesome until I'd blown out my knee our sophomore year and she'd broken her ankle our junior year which had ended both our athletic careers. Afterward, our teammates referred to us as the Gimp Sisters which we couldn't dispute.

I closed her door and blowing out a breath as I walked to the front door, decided to go find out if my dream future was to be.

~*~*~*~

"What would you do?" I asked Gladys (yes, Gladys), Sharee and my other best friend from high school who was now in New York attending the Fashion Institute of Technology. She'd been an amazing designer even in high school, having made my prom dress our senior year which had been fabulous, and after three years at Hallervan, she'd been accepted to the Institute and was now following her dream hoping to become famous someday. We missed her but we talked so often, it was almost like she was here anyway.

"I'd go for it, of course! Grow some fucking balls, Frankie!" she answered with a giggle. Where Sharee was the realist and I was the dreamer, Gladys had always been the crazy party girl up for anything and I'd known she'd say that.

"Easy for you to say, Glad. You're a blond bombshell packing a killer bod and fuck me eyes."

This made her giggle more. "Oh, Frankie. When will you realize how gorgeous you are? Sophia Loren's got nothing on you, girl! This guy'd be a fool not to fall for you."

I rolled my eyes. "So you think Sharee was right? I should do this? Just go up, ring his doorbell and ask him out?"

"Hell yeah! And like I said, if he doesn't take you up on it, he's a dumbass."

"All right. If this doesn't go well, Sharee's buying at O'Leary's tonight and when you come home for spring break, you're taking me to Spinasse."

"You're on. And, listen, honey. It's not the end of the world if it doesn't work out with this guy, yeah? You're beautiful and deserve the best so you hold your head high."

I'd just turned into Ryker's neighborhood and felt my pulse start racing. "I don't know, Glad. I don't think I can do this."

"You can! You're just asking him to coffee. No big deal, right?"

"Right," I whispered as I pulled up in front of his house and parked in the same spot I'd been the morning before. "Will you at least stay on the phone with me for a minute?"

"Of course. Deep breaths." When I didn't say anything, Gladys called, "Frank?"

"I'm here."

"What're you doing?"

"Breathing."

She laughed. "That's enough. Go!"

I closed my eyes and reached for the door handle. "I can't believe I'm doing this," I said when I got out and faced the house.

"Wait!" she yelled scaring the bajeebus out of me.

"What?" I hissed, automatically hunching down trying to hide behind my car as if she was there and had seen something.

"What're you wearing?"

I huffed out an annoyed laugh as I stood straight again. "God! Don't fucking do that! You scared the shit outta me!" When my heart stopped trying to claw its way out of my chest, I answered, "I'm wearing black jeans..."

"Flares or leggings?"

"Skinny. And the burgundy blouse you made for me last year."

"Nice! What jacket?"

"My army green pea coat."

"Shoes?"

"Black ankle boots."

"You go, girl! Go get your man!"

I shook my head before taking a breath and blowing it out, still holding the phone to my ear. "Here goes nothing."

Walking up the drive toward the house on wobbly legs I wondered why I'd agreed to do this. But as I took in the cute little house in front of me, I knew why. It was for the preservation of my and my children's future.

"Where are you?" Gladys whispered.

"I'm in the driveway. Almost at the walk to go to the front door. Between a blue pickup truck and a hot pink VW Beetle."

"Okay."

A few seconds passed.

"You there yet?"

"No."

"Why not?"

"I think my feet are stuck."

She chuckled. "I'm right here. Go!"

I took another step and that's when the front door opened and I froze.

"Fuck," I whispered.

"What?"

"Fuck!" I now whisper-hissed, standing there like a statue hoping I wouldn't be seen, you know, right out there in the open in broad daylight and all.

"What?" she asked even louder.

Oh, my God.

Ryker had come out onto the front porch in jeans and was shirtless but that wasn't the "Oh, my God" part.

"What's going on?" Gladys whispered.

But I couldn't answer as I stood there, almost half hidden by the blue truck watching as Ryker made out with a platinum blond woman who was built like a fucking stripper, meaning she was hot. And when I say "made out," I mean, practically screwing her right there on the porch, grabbing her ass and grinding himself all up on her.

Fuck!

Fuck!

"Frankie!"

"Hang on!" I snapped into my phone.

And that's when Ryker heard me and pried his lips off the chick and looked my way.

Fuck, fuck, fuck!

"Can I help you?" he asked, narrowing his eyes at me, watching me as if I was exactly the Peeping Tom I was.

I immediately dropped my phone into my jacket pocket and decided to go with the first thing that popped into my head. "Uh, I, uh saw this Beetle and, uh, I love the color, so I was, um, trying to get a better look at it."

Shit.

Shit!

"That's mine!" the blonde answered with a giggle, then tiptoeing up and giving Ryker one last kiss she turned and walked toward me on heels that would've broken my ankles, calling back to him over her shoulder, "Call me, baby." When she got to me, she said, "My dad got this for me because he knows it's my favorite color. Oh! I'm Lindsey!"

"Hi. Uh, Frankie."

She giggled, cocking her head to her shoulder. "No kidding?"

"No kidding."

"Awesome! Well, I need to go but I live over on Elm across from the university. You're more than welcome to look me up and I'll let you drive it sometime!"

God. And she was nice too. Ergh.

"Thanks. I'll, um, definitely look you up."

"'Kay! See ya!" She opened her car door, blew Ryker a kiss over the top of it, got in and started it while I stood watching it all. She waved to me as she backed down the drive and once in the street drove off.

"I know you," I heard from right behind me which made me jump a foot in the air.

I turned around quickly to face the freaking Greek god that stood there, seeing that his hair, cut in what my mom would call a curtain cut undercut (she was a hairdresser), was all messy but looking sexy as hell. Shaved sides and longer on top and let me tell you, Ryker worked that hair well. Then there was his amazing tattooed chest and cut abs that were on display for my viewing pleasure. And, dear God, that damned V just below his waist that was so prominent and disappeared inside the jeans that hung low on his hips literally had my mouth drooling.

"Uh, no, I don't think you do," I mumbled not able to control my eyes as they roamed over his hard body. God!

"I think I do."

My eyes shot up and locked with his light brown ones that I just noticed had gold flecks and were lined in dark, sooty lashes. Dammit. Why'd he have to look so good?

"No, I don't think so," I muttered again, starting to back away from him because I needed to get the hell out of there now since it'd just dawned on me that he and hot pink Beetle owner Lindsey had spent the night together and that wasn't cool.

His eyes were intense practically boring a hole right through me watching as I took another step back which only led to his taking a barefooted one forward.

"Yeah. I do," he repeated, his eyes full of recognition now.

Shit!

"Sorry, I don't think you do," I repeated and turned to go.

The next thing I knew, he moved fast and had me backed against the truck, his hands on either side of me on the truck bed, keeping me there as I looked up at him with big eyes. Damn.

"You were here Saturday," he informed me of something I already knew.

I licked my lips nervously wondering how the hell I could get free, contemplating whether he could sue me if I stomped on his foot with my boot before making a run for it. I made a note to ask Sharee about it. But no way was I going to stand there and relive something that had meant nothing to him just to be humiliated all over again.

Leaning in close he said, "I fucked you," all low and sexy and hot, his gorgeous eyes still piercing mine. "You were the hungry one who couldn't get enough of my dick. Practically starved."

Now wait just a damned minute here. "Wh-what?" I asked indignantly, shocked that he'd talk that way to me. And *about* me!

"Yeah, babe. Tightest, wettest pussy I've had. Possibly best piece of ass I think I've ever had."

My mouth fell open. "Did you really just say that?" I glared up at him.

"I think you heard me." Now I saw amusement in those captivating eyes of his and that really pissed me off.

Oh. My. God.

Oh, my God!

I pushed at his chest and ducked out under his arm spinning to face him, my hands going to my hips. "You're unbelievable!" I spat, glowering at him.

"If I recall right, that's what you were moaning the other night." He gave me a half smirk and it was all I could do to keep from smacking the shit out of him.

"You've *got* to be kidding me." I gave him my best repulsed look. "To think I've wanted you for two years. And now I find out you're just some..." I threw my hand out at him as I frowned in disgust, "some crude asshole who'll fuck any *piece of ass* you can find! God! How stupid am I?" I turned and stomped down the driveway to my car.

"Not just *any* piece of ass, baby!" he hollered after me. "Only the hottest pieces for me!" I heard him chuckling as I jerked open my car door and got inside slamming my door.

I turned the key to start the engine and took off as fast as my poor little Camry would let me, giving him one last glare only to see him still smirking at me, his arms now across his magnificent chest.

"Frankie!" I heard coming from my coat pocket.

Shit! I hadn't hung up when I'd dropped my phone into it.

I dug it out of my pocket and brought it to my ear, too pissed to care that I was risking being pulled over. "Did you hear that?" I screeched at Gladys.

"I did! Oh, my God! Frankie! He sounds so hot!" she squealed.

What?

"Are you kidding me right now? Did you not just hear what he said about me?"

"Yes! That's what was hot!"

"Glad! He was making out with another woman! He fucked her last night! The night after he fucked me!" I couldn't help but scream now.

"Calm down, Frankie."

"Calm down? Seriously?"

"Yes."

Wow. Had everyone gone nuts in the last twenty minutes? I brought my phone down to Bluetooth it as I focused on evening out my breathing. Okay. She was right. I definitely needed to calm down. Jesus.

"Are you calm now?"

I rolled my eyes. "I guess," I bit out.

"You like this guy."

"*Liked*," I answered, making sure to put emphasis on the "D."

"Okay, liked. And up until about twenty minutes ago he was your dream guy, right?"

More eye rolling, more biting out. "Yes."

"So what's changed?"

"Really?"

"Yeah, really."

"Gladys, he fucked another woman!"

"So he's a guy with lots of testosterone. Are you guys dating? Nope. So it's not like he was cheating on you! You think he's been celibate all this time just waiting for you to come to him?"

She had a point. I guessed. "But he was supposed to be my future husband," I said quietly, trying to come to terms with what had just happened.

"And you wanted your future husband to be a virgin?"

I blew out a breath. "I don't know why you're on his side."

"You know I'm always on your side. I just want you to see how silly you're being."

"Whatever. If you went to see Nathan Bogle to start your life together and caught him making out with some hot stripper chick, you'd be pissed too!"

I heard her gasp. Ah, I knew that'd open her eyes. "You're right. Shit! I get it now! I'm so sorry!"

I chuckled before answering resignedly, "It's okay. So my dream was bashed two days in a row. Time to get a new one, don't you think?" The backs of my eyes burned and I had to blink several times to keep the tears from coming just thinking how stupid I'd been. "God, I'm such an idiot."

"No, you're not. And from what that guy said I'm not so sure your dream's over just yet."

"What?" I asked on a disbelieving huff.

"He said you were the best he's had, Frankie."

Now I huffed out a humorless laugh. "I'll bet he's had so many how would he know? You eat enough cream puffs, they're bound to start tasting the same, Glad."

"Well, apparently he likes the cream in your puff."

"You didn't."

She laughed. "I did. But mark my words, Frankie. He's not finished with you yet."

"He has no choice because I'm finished with him," I retorted.

And I really hoped I meant it.

I had only two classes this semester including my student teaching seminar which would meet periodically throughout the semester as well as two days this week (that was where I was headed now) then I'd begin fourteen weeks of student teaching. I was excited because I'd be teaching seven weeks of English and seven of PE in two separate schools and I couldn't wait to get started. I'd also enrolled in Care and Prevention of Athletic Injuries which met on Monday and Wednesday nights in the training room of the fieldhouse. I'd taken it on a whim thinking that if I ever decided to coach a high school sport I'd need it, so what the heck.

Today's seminar lasted just under an hour and now I was in line to sign in and pick up my packet.

"Frankie!"

I turned and saw my friend Shelby walking up.

"Hey, Shelby. You ready for this?" I grinned at her. She was an elementary education major and wanted to teach first grade. We'd met in our College Algebra class freshman year and from the beginning I'd known she had to be majoring in something that dealt with children because she was a ball of energy who'd be perfect working with little kids.

"I am! I can't wait to get to teach those little babies! They're all so cute and sweet at that age!"

I snorted. "By the time they get to me, they're all jaded and tired of school."

She chuckled. "I just love the innocence of the little ones. I don't know why you want to deal with older kids."

"I don't know why you like the little ones. I swear, if I taught that age and a kid peed his pants or wanted me to wipe his snotty nose, I think I'd puke."

She cracked up. "Oh, now, it's not that bad! You must not have any younger brothers or sisters."

"Nope. Only child and spoiled rotten." I winked at her.

We chatted a bit more waiting our turn.

"Francesca Mangenelli," I told the woman sitting behind the table when I made it to the front.

"That's a mouthful," a guy said from behind me.

I laughed as I turned around to remark to him, "It is. Try learning how to spell it when you're in kindergar—" And I froze.

Holy shit. Ryker Powers was standing right behind me. And he was giving me his sexy half grin. Gah!

"So, Francesca Mangenelli. I'm Ryker Powers. It's nice to meet you." Keeping his eyes on mine, he took my hand that hung limply at my side in his huge one and squeezed it gently, and all I could do was stand staring into his golden eyes that were dancing with amusement.

"Wow," I heard Shelby whisper from beside me which suddenly snapped me out of my daze.

Raising an eyebrow at him and with a coy smile, I slipped my hand from his.

"Ms. Mangenelli?" the woman behind the desk said.

I looked back to her. "Yes?"

"Your packet." I took it from her and turned to go only to hear her sharply say, "You need to sign off that you received it, young lady."

"Oh, yes, sorry," I mumbled as I took the pen and signed my name. When I finished, I looked at Shelby. "I've got to go. I'll see you around." I gave Ryker my best sarcastic smirk and took off.

That night in Care and Prevention of Athletic Injuries had been fun. Coach Nolan, the football team's athletic trainer, was the teacher and he'd shown us videos on taping with kinesiology and zinc oxide tape, told us to look in our textbooks and had us partner up and tape each other's ankles. As an athlete, I'd been taped before, but now I was cursing myself for not paying much attention at the time. Taylor, the girl I'd teamed up with, said she'd also been an athlete and had been taped before, but now she and I looked at each other nervously since we were in the same boat. Sadly, our attempts had our ankles looking somewhat like a mummy's. Coach Nolan had walked by our table, raised an eyebrow at our shoddy attempts, looked at me then Taylor then back at each ankle and had given a "Humph" before moving on. We'd cracked up.

Before class was over, Coach had informed us he'd be bringing in athletes Wednesday night for us to practice on. I'd talked to Ciara and Madison from the basketball team and they said they'd be there, so I hoped I got one of them which would make taping less stressful. I'd really enjoyed the class, though, and actually learned a lot in just the one night.

~*~*~*~

"He wants you," Sharee said over the top of her beer mug. She'd made good on her promise to take me to O'Leary's if I'd gotten embarrassed when I'd gone by Ryker's which was a mammoth understatement since I'd been completely mortified.

"Apparently he wants every woman," I replied sardonically.

I'd run into Chance Reynolds, star quarterback for the football team and who Sharee had recently broken things off with, after class and asked him about Ryker. Of course, I didn't tell her I'd talked to him. I wasn't stupid. Plus, I didn't want to get cussed out by her. Anyway,

Chance had informed me that Ryker was considered a god amongst the athletes on campus because of all his sexual exploits which had made me all kinds of grossed out.

"He's a hot guy. I'm sure women throw themselves at him all the time. What's he gonna say? No?" she challenged.

I took a sip of my Lazy Eye, a drink with Jim Beam, having made sure to take advantage of Sharee's offer to take me out for drinks by ordering something I liked that was more expensive than beer. Hey, she could afford it since both her parents were attorneys and she'd be one soon and probably working in the same firm they did bringing in a gazillion dollars a year. I set my tumbler down and eyed her. "He could take a night or two off every now and then."

She snorted. "I'm sure he does, Frank. I'll bet if you went by his place in the morning, no one would be there."

"Oh, no, you don't. I'm not falling for that shit again. My luck, I'd see him making out with triplets on his front porch." I narrowed my eyes at her which made her chuckle. "At least Gladys understands."

"It's not that I don't understand," she scoffed making me squint my eyes now. "I get it. I do. I mean, Chance totally taught me not to trust any man ever. Fucker." She downed the rest of her beer and signaled to the waitress that we needed another.

"So how'd your class go tonight?" I asked, veering away from that particularly touchy topic. Sharee thought Chance had cheated but I honestly didn't. As the quarterback, he'd had to do a photo shoot with one of the cheerleaders for the program cover. The shoot had lasted longer than Sharee thought it should have and she'd immediately cried, "Personal foul!" at this, not even giving him the opportunity to explain. As her best friend, I'd listened to her complaint and tried presenting reasons for the shoot's delay but she'd wanted nothing to do with it, so I'd given up deciding she must've wanted to break from him to begin with.

"Philosophy of Law? It was good. We have assigned readings we'll discuss. This week's is the death penalty. Good times."

The waitress brought our drinks and I asked Sharee before taking a sip, "So what's your take?"

"If they're guilty," she made a *squick* noise as she drew her finger across her throat.

"Well, all right," I replied with a giggle.

I managed to steer our conversation away from Ryker the rest of the night, thank God, and since we both had class in the morning, we had only one more drink before calling a cab to take us back to our apartment.

I managed to avoid Ryker the next morning in seminar. Oh, I'd seen him all right, how could I not notice the hottest guy there, but I was proud of how I'd played it off and looked right past him as if he wasn't even there. Shelby had been full of questions but I just told her he was someone from my past who was going to stay there and left it at that.

After seminar, I'd been bored to tears at home since I'd quit my job at the downtown Nordstrom, which I'd loved by the way since I'd worked in handbags and accessories and getting to handle all the designer purses all day. But I knew student teaching would take up most of my time, so I ended up cleaning out my closet and dresser, taking the clothes I knew I'd no longer wear and dropping them off at Goodwill. I'd felt so good about getting rid of things that I'd gone shopping for new clothes, totally negating my progress. Oh, well.

The next morning I was psyched, ready to get to the school I'd been assigned where I'd be teaching elementary PE the first seven weeks which was awesome. My mentor teacher was Coach Gilbert, a crotchety but hilarious guy who'd been the football coach at one of the area high schools for umpteen years before retiring. He now taught PE because he said his wife had told him he was driving her crazy being at home all day and if he didn't get back to doing something, she'd kick him out and/or divorce him. I thought it was crazy how well the kids responded to him since he was rather harsh with them, but there was no denying the mutual love they had for each other. He may have acted as if he was annoyed when each class came in, but the twinkle in his eyes told a different story.

I'd had a blast helping "coach" the kids that day but had been shocked when Coach G had split his first hour, which was made up of first graders, into teams and had them play dodge ball. Four kids had had to sit out because they'd gotten beaned in the face and were crying, two had fallen down and scraped their knees and had to go to the nurse to get Band-Aids and one unfortunate boy had taken a ball to his crotch which made him howl in pain.

"Um, Coach? You don't think this is a bit much for kids this little?" I'd asked after one kid ran over with a bloody nose only to have Coach G tell him to suck it up and go to the bathroom and get a paper towel.

"Girl, these kids need this more than anything right now. Kids are so babied nowadays it makes me sick. And give them a few years and they'll be on their cell phones twenty-four seven or sitting inside all summer long playing video games getting even softer. I'm teaching them to be tough and to appreciate sports. The ones who can hack it will be the future stars," he informed me.

I didn't understand his logic but when class was over, they all gathered around him (even the hurt ones) telling him how much fun they'd had and could they do it again tomorrow. Maybe he had a point. Who knew?

The rest of the day had been the same only with older kids who loved Coach G as much as the little ones did. I guess he had a system and it worked, so who was I to question it? By the end of the day, I'd learned quite a bit and knew I was going to like it and couldn't wait until the next week when he'd told me I'd be taking over a couple classes.

That night I was back in my athletic injury class, watching yet another video on taping as we waited for the athletes to get there for us to practice on. I knew Ciara and Madison and several other basketball players from the women's and men's teams were coming, but what Coach Nolan had failed to mention was he was also bringing in volunteers from the wrestling team since they were in season too. Yeah. I didn't find this out until the door opened and several muscular guys walked in.

And when Ryker was among them my eyes just about popped out of my head.

What the hell? The wrestlers had had a meet today but I guessed it was now over.

"Fuck," I mumbled.

"What?" Taylor, my partner from Monday, asked.

"Tell you later," I whispered, leaning my head to her and rolling my eyes.

I got brave and took another look at Ryker in all his brooding intensity. And holy shit, he was hot!

His dark caramel-colored hair was still wet from the shower he'd just taken and the gray compression shirt he wore stretched across his sculpted chest clinging to his stomach to where if I wanted, I could probably count every ab muscle he had. All eight of them.

Damn.

His eyes immediately met mine and the smirk he gave me had me frowning. I frowned even harder when he made a beeline right to me.

"Y-you aren't who I'm working with," I sputtered when he came up to my table which now got me his grin.

"Coach Nolan?" he hollered. "I'm with Francesca. You good with that?"

"I'm good, Ryker. Tell her you're a groin strain," Coach Nolan hollered back as he walked around the room assigning athletes to everyone.

Groin strain? What! Was he serious? Oh, my God.

"This is so not cool," I hissed, glaring at Ryker who was already getting onto the table with a huge shit-eating grin on his face.

"So, gorgeous, you want me to drop trou or just hike my shorts up?" he asked, and believe it or not, his grin got even bigger.

"I hate you," I muttered as I bent under the table to grab some KT tape out of the caddie.

"Didn't hate me last Saturday when I made you come so many times you were speakin' in fuckin' tongues."

I stood up slowly and gave him the most hateful look I could. "That was before I knew you were an asshole." This made him snort. "And a manwhore."

He threw his head back and barked out a laugh and I'll be damned if that wasn't the most attractive thing I've ever seen. Ugh.

"You didn't seem to mind my 'manwhore' skills the other night, darlin'," he said still chuckling.

I set the tape on the table and turned to him. "Here's the deal. I'll do this but you have to shut up."

"I'll try," he answered, a half smirk now gracing his beautiful face.

"Whatever," I mumbled as I looked down at the tape knowing I'd have to measure it. When my eyes came up I saw his dancing with amusement because he knew my dilemma. God! "Hang on."

I opened my book to the page that illustrated taping groins and cringed. Okay. I could do this. Blowing out a breath, I grabbed the tape and moved toward him.

"I need you to bend your knee to create a stretch in the, uh, the groin area." He pulled his knee up slightly on the leg farther from me hanging the one close to me off the table. I licked my lips as I tried figuring out how to do this without having to touch him. "Okay, I need to measure. Keep quiet." I lifted my eyes and watched as with sheer glee on his face, he lifted a hand, put it to his mouth as if he had a key in it, turned it and threw the "key" away. Ass.

Moving in between his legs, I held the end of the tape putting it on the inside of his leg a few inches above the back of his knee stretching it up and over his muscular thigh toward his crotch. Gah! I next quickly stepped away letting go of the tape as I grabbed the scissors. This, of course, made me lose my measurement, so gritting my teeth I glanced up at him and held the tape out toward him as if it was all his fault.

"I've got to get the right amount or it won't work," I accused, inwardly rolling my eyes because of course it wasn't his fault he was so distracting. It was mine for being so mesmerized by such a jerk.

"You need me to give you something long to measure it by?"

Just when I thought he couldn't get any more disconcerting... but now I snickered because this shit had to end. I was tired of being in a constant flustered state when I was near him.

"What?" he asked, narrowing his eyes at me.

"Nothing. Just, thanks for the offer but I just need something more than six inches to go by."

Another barked laugh. "Baby, you know you need to double that if we're being totally honest here."

I huffed out a humorless chuckle but the bad thing was he wasn't totally wrong, having only exaggerated by maybe three inches. Cocky jerk.

"Whatever," I murmured again as I went in to measure once more.

"Whoa there, *cara*," he said, suddenly grabbing my hand making me look up at him with a frown. "You need to set those scissors down first before you get close to Ryker, Jr."

I laughed despite the fact that he'd just called me *precious* in Italian which was what my grandpa had always called me, knowing Ryker probably had no clue what it meant anyway. Setting the scissors down, I gave him an *am I good now* look and proceeded to measure the tape again.

"You don't even know what *cara* means," I challenged trying to divert my attention away from the fact that I was mere inches from his glorious cock.

Before I could move back, he wrapped an arm around my waist pulling me to him and as he looked deep into my eyes, he answered, "It means *precious*."

My eyes got big as I stared at him, shocked as hell that he'd known.

"Um, yeah," was all I could squeak out before I pulled away making him let me go. Lord. Why was I so attracted to this guy? I mean, besides the obvious, of course. But I knew he was a player. Knew he only wanted to sleep with me because, hell, he slept with everyone. And remembering that pissed me off, so after cutting the tape, I tried announcing indifferently, "You're going to have to pull your shorts leg up," but I'm sure my voice cracked.

"Sure you don't want me to just take them off?" he asked, his lip curling up on one side.

I found myself sighing yet again as I looked back at him. He really was beautiful. Too bad he had no depth of character when it came to relationships.

"Just pull it up," I directed, feeling as if I were talking to one of the first graders I'd helped coach today.

Placing the tape on his knee and stretching it up was the most tedious thing ever since I knew where it'd end. But, by golly, I did it and couldn't help the triumphant look I gave him.

"Good job, Mangenelli," Coach Nolan said as he walked by. He added over his shoulder, "Now add another piece just like that just above it and you'll be done."

"Shit," I mumbled beneath my breath.

"What was that?" Ryker asked with a snort.

I gave him my evil death glare as I grabbed the KT tape to cut a new piece. Once done, I stepped between his legs again to apply it

"I'm thinking I should pay you when you're finished," he smarted off.

I've always had somewhat of a bad temper which at that moment I demonstrated, immediately feeling horrible afterward.

"What the fuck?" Ryker shouted when I ripped the second piece of tape off his leg after having smoothed it down, probably pulling off lots of leg hair with it.

But I had to own it now. Giving him a sheepish look, I said, "Sorry." I smoothed it all back down and was finished, thank God.

His voice dropped to a menacingly low level. "Gonna make you pay for that one, *Mangenelli*."

My eyes came up to his as I bit my lip actually feeling bad that I'd hurt him. "I said I was sorry."

He narrowed his eyes at me. "You owe me now. After class, you're coming home with me to kiss this shit all better."

I huffed out a laugh. "Right. And after I'm finished I'll blow you to show how deeply apologetic I am." I rolled my eyes.

His mouth was slightly open and askew and I watched in fascination as his tongue touched the molars on the bottom left. "I'd love for that smartassed mouth of yours to be wrapped around my cock again." He was glaring at me but it was kind of sexy. Can glaring even *be* sexy? And I thought I figured out that the tongue thing was him being mad and probably trying to keep from yelling at me, kind of like gritting his teeth, I guessed. But even that was sexy. Argh!

Trying to act annoyed, I retorted, "That'll be happening never."

"It will. And after it does, I'm gonna spank your heart-shaped ass for being a bad girl tonight," he said low.

My mouth dropped open as I ignored the gush of wetness between my legs at his threat. "You're kidding, right?" I returned with a frown.

He shook his head slowly as his eyes burned into mine. "Thing is, I know you'll like it too."

My frown got even, well, frownier. "I highly doubt it," I scoffed.

He leaned in closer, his fingers encircling my wrist as he pulled me toward him. "Wanna know why I know?"

I couldn't help it. I nodded.

"When I said I'd spank you, your breathing sped up, your eyes dilated and you suddenly looked flushed. Bet if I stuck my hand in your panties I'd find you're dripping wet right now." He put his mouth to my ear and whispered, "Am I wrong, Francesca?"

Holy hell.

"Stop calling me that," I replied shakily, flustered beyond all measure. No one called me by my full name except Mrs. Bertolini and Grandma and Grandpa Mangenelli, and it was unsettling to hear Ryker call me it.

He let my wrist go and pulled back, a smirk gracing his gorgeous face as if he'd found out a deep, dark secret or something.

"All right! Students, put your materials away and I'll come by to grade you," Coach Nolan called.

I watched as Ryker smoothed the tape down and saw that there actually was hair stuck to it that was making the end curl up. God. I was a horrible person.

"I'm really sorry I did that," I whispered.

He looked up at me, eyes narrowed. "Oh, you'll pay, babe."

And that's what I was afraid of.

5—Penalty

Sometimes I question my ability at making good decisions.

I say this because I was now sitting across from Ryker at O'Leary's. Yep. But I wasn't totally going to take the blame for how it happened.

Right before Coach Nolan had come by to give me my grade, Ryker had basically blackmailed me.

"You want a good grade, go out with me tonight. Otherwise, I'll show Coach the chunk of hair you ripped off my leg."

I'd narrowed my eyes at him wondering if he was bluffing but from the look on his face, I knew he wasn't. I shook my head. "You're unreal."

"You have no idea." He grinned. "Oh wait. I guess you do."

Oh, dear God. At that moment I thanked my lucky stars for my Italian ancestry since my blushing didn't show up too much.

"Why, Ms. Mangenelli, are you blushing?"

Damn it. I guess I was wrong.

"No! I don't blush!"

God. The looks he could give. And this one had me melting right there in front of him.

"Lemme take a look, Frankie," Coach Nolan said just then.

I glanced at Ryker who raised his eyebrows at me in question, his hand on the tape. Crap! All I could do was nod, agreeing to going out with him.

"She did a great job, Coach. Very professional and knew what she was doing," Ryker said.

I choked out a cough making Coach Nolan look at me, his eyebrows raised too.

"Is that so?" he asked. Again, all I could do was nod. "All right. Looks like a solid *B*," he muttered, noticing Ryker's hand holding the top part down. "Class is over. See you next Monday." He walked away to look at the next student's work.

Ryker turned letting both legs hang off the table. "Come with me to the locker room so I can get dressed."

I bit my lip thinking I could just tell him no. I mean, I'd already gotten a good grade.

"Not gonna chicken out, are you?" His eyes challenged me to turn him down as he stood.

"No. Of course not." He knew I was an athlete which meant if I was anything, I was as competitive as they came, so with a deep sigh, I followed him out of the training room.

I'd waited outside the locker room for him to change and now here we were at O'Leary's.

As we waited for the waitress to bring our beers, I'd sat uncomfortably not knowing what to say, but Ryker sat back against the booth, one arm thrown over it lazily as he watched me fidgeting. Of course he wasn't uneasy. As cool as he was, he'd probably feel right at home in a police line-up. And knowing him, he'd try to come off as the guilty party just to mess with them.

I took a drink before clearing my throat wanting to break what I thought was an awkward silence. "I was here just the other night with my roommate."

He took a drink and I watched, captivated at how his Adam's apple moved up and down the column of his neck. Then I reminded myself that he disgusted me and I looked away.

"Yeah?"

"Yeah," I answered, turning to gaze around the place as I took another drink.

"You're doing your student teaching." It was a statement rather than a question.

I turned back to him and nodded. "You're doing yours too?"

He nodded now and we sat there in more silence as I took in more of the bar.

Well, this was going swimmingly. I picked up my bottle and took a sip and setting it on the table replied, "Well, this has been an exceedingly stimulating exchange and all, but I really do have things to do."

"I like you, Francesca."

I sat back against the booth kind of in shock because it wasn't like we were chatting each other up. "You don't even know me."

I watched as one side of his mouth went up. "I do. But I'd like to get to know you better."

Here came the blush again since I knew to what he was referring.

I licked my lips. "That was a mistake."

"You think so?"

"Well, yeah."

"Why?"

"Why?"

"Yeah, why?"

I took another drink and moving my eyes to him saw his eyebrow go up.

"Do I make you uncomfortable?" he asked.

I huffed out a despondent laugh. "Yes."

He scrunched his face innocently, which was too cute, as he jerked his head back. "Really?"

I let out another humorless chuckle in response to this while his prying eyes regarded me as I squirmed a bit in the booth, not wanting to explain. But then I thought why not. So taking a deep breath, I revealed practically all. "For two years I've, uh, watched you." And seeing how he was giving me a *that's too creepy for words* look I rushed to explain. "I saw you our sophomore year. I played basketball but when I hurt my knee I was done. That gave me time during practice when I was just sitting around watching to watch, um, other things." I stared at the coaster I'd picked up, flipping it over in my hand a few times.

"And?"

God. I should've just kept my big mouth shut. I gazed up at him under my lashes only to see him still watching me intensely. Ack! I took another drink finishing off my beer and set the bottle on the table, looking anywhere but at him.

"And, Francesca?"

I glanced back at him only to see the waitress placing another beer in front of me. "Oh, thanks," I said, looking up at her. She smiled and nodded before walking away. I downed three-quarters of my beer in several gulps hoping my stalling would make him move on to another topic.

"Hey," I heard him say quietly and saw him grin when I gave him a questioning look as if I didn't know what we were talking about. "Continue," he ordered dipping his head toward me.

Okay. The sooner I got this over with the quicker I could go home. "I'm a dreamer." There. That ought to do it. But his annoyed head tilt he gave me made me continue. "Sharee, my best friend, gets mad because she says I dream too much, that I come up with scenarios that are unrealistic and I guess she's right." I shrugged.

"So you dreamed about me?" God. I used to think his smirks were kind of hot but now I knew better.

"Yeah, Ryker, I did. That is until I knew what a gigolo you are."

He snorted out a laugh. "Gigolo?"

I frowned. "Yeah. You know, dog, libertine, *manwhore*."

"Baby, I'm a guy. Guys like sex. Lots of it. If there are women out there willing to give it, not gonna turn it down." He shrugged as he shook his head and pursed his lips in a matter of fact way.

Ugh.

"I guess not since you've probably slept with the entire female populace of Seattle."

"There are a few I haven't pursued." He winked and I was done.

I scooted toward the end of my booth. "Well, this has been fun and all, but I need to go home."

He was up and on his feet faster than I could make it out, blocking me in the booth.

"I need to go," I snapped, glowering up at him.

Putting his finger into the front of the waistband of my jeans he pulled me closer, bending his head and whispered, "Stay." And then he kissed me.

~*~*~*~

I was officially an idiot.

After we'd kissed, Ryker had pulled his wallet out of his back pocket, thrown a couple twenties on the table, grabbed my hand and pulled me out of O'Leary's to the parking lot. After we made out against his truck for a while, he'd talked me into following him to his house which hadn't taken much convincing.

Shit. Idiot.

Now we were in his bedroom.

In his bed.

Making out hardcore.

Coats on the floor. Shoes thrown wherever.

His hard body on top of mine felt like heaven as he ground his hips into me and God help me but I wanted him badly. So when he sat up, pulling me up with him to remove my shirt, I didn't resist. I also didn't make a fuss when he unhooked my bra, slowly slipping the straps down my arms and pulling it off.

"Fucking beautiful," he murmured before laying me back and taking one of my nipples into his mouth and sucking hard.

"Oh, God," I moaned as he moved to my other breast, giving it the same attention which made me bow up off the bed as I dug my fingers into his shoulders.

When he sat back on his knees, his hands went to my jeans unbuttoning them and sliding them and my panties down my legs, his eyes practically luminescent as he looked down at my exposed body.

"You're stunning, Francesca," he muttered as he took me in.

But he was the stunning one, his hair mussed from my fingers tangling in it, the scruff on his chin making him appear even more dangerous than I knew he already was. And I so knew this wasn't smart. Knew I was going to get my heart broken. Yeah, he'd said he liked me but I'm sure he "liked" a lot of women. But did that stop me? Hell no.

Nope, stupid me sat up and tugged at the hem of his t-shirt pulling it up and over his head then keeping my eyes on all the ink on his chest, the abs that looked chiseled into his abdomen, my hands slid down to his jeans to unbutton them. And slipping a hand inside, I wrapped it around his hard cock making him groan which made me smirk (for a change) at having made him feel good.

"You like my cock don't you, baby. Like I said, starving," he groaned. Before I could argue, he'd grabbed the outsides of my thighs pulling me up which made me release my hold on him as I fell back onto the bed and then his face moved between my legs and I felt his lips against me.

"Ryker!" I screamed because his mouth and then his tongue were exactly where I needed them making it impossible for me to control all the moaning I was doing as he sucked and licked, taking me so high I swear I was seeing stars.

"That's it. Come on my face. Soak my chin, baby."

Oh, my God.

That was all it took and I was there, shouting out my climax as my knees clamped against the sides of his head. Damn.

I was breathing heavily, tremors still zinging through my body, when he stood looking intensely down at me and cupped his chin as if in thought. I didn't know what he was doing until he moved his straightened pointer finger up his chin to his mouth where I saw him suck my juices off of it.

"Sweetest I've ever tasted," he remarked, giving me a look that burned right through me before bending to pull off his jeans and boxer briefs.

Holy hell.

He next got a condom out of the nightstand and put it on, and was now standing in all his gorgeous nudity looking down at me as if trying to figure out what to do with me, the whole while stroking his huge length which sent another spasm through my body. Good lord.

"Spread your legs for me, baby," he finally said putting a knee on the bed. I did as I was told watching him move his body over mine, and putting his forearm on the side of my head he ran his other hand up my throat and grasped my chin with his fingers before leaning down to kiss me hard and wet and deep. "Can't wait to be inside you again," he growled as he pulled back and looping his arm behind my knee he drew his hips back and plunged inside making me cry out.

His strokes were strong and measure and from the moment he started moving I felt everything building again. Fast. Oh my. The next thing I knew, I was coming again. God.

"Yeah. Just like that, Francesca. Love feeling you pulsing around me, gripping me tight. So fuckin' starved, baby."

I was about to protest again (because I may have been starved for his body but he did *not* have to keep bringing it up) when I lost him as he flipped me over onto my belly, drew my hips up with his rough hands and sank inside deep before I could catch my breath.

"So fuckin' wet," he growled as he slammed inside, his hips now pistoning against my bottom.

I buried my face in the mattress, my hands clenching the sheet as mewls of pleasure escaped my mouth but suddenly I let out a yelp because he'd smacked my butt.

What in the world?

"Told you I was gonna spank you for being a bad girl," he ground out before striking me again.

"Oh… God," I moaned because, damn it, that was hot.

"Knew you'd get off on this," he uttered, giving me one last spank.

And he was so right. Wow.

He rubbed his hand over my bottom a couple times as if to soothe me before sliding it up the middle of my back where he wrapped my hair in his hand and tugged my head back. His mouth was then right at my ear where he prompted, "Tell me I'm right." He didn't wait for my answer as he slammed his hard length inside, burying himself deep. When I still didn't answer, could only pant, he jerked his hips back before thrusting in so hard he bottomed out at my cervix.

"Oh, my God!" I cried.

"Tell me," he demanded as he pulled out then slammed back in again.

"Yes! Yes! You're right!" I yelled out as another orgasm blasted through me. Holy Jesus.

"Fuck!" he roared as he came, driving in several times, his hips slapping against my bottom until his movements stopped and he planted himself deep resting his forehead on the back of my shoulder, his heavy breaths puffing against my skin.

We lay that way for several minutes before he released my hair and snaked his hand around where he gripped my chin with his fingers, turning my face to his then leaned in to kiss me hard.

"Be right back," he said against my lips. He let my chin go but kissed my shoulder as he withdrew then he was gone.

I was content to stay put because my entire body felt like it was boneless and I was trembling like crazy. When he came back, I felt him push his hands underneath me, then turning me in his arms he picked me up.

"Are you cold?" he asked as I continued shivering in his arms.

"N-no," I answered through rattling teeth. Jeez.

I saw the amusement in his eyes before he whispered, "See you're worn out." He kissed my forehead before pulling back the bedcovers laying me in his bed, and after turning out the lamp on the nightstand, he got in beside me, pulling me into his arms where I buried my face in his neck as he held me tightly.

And now the doubt set in.

What had I been thinking? I mean, don't get me wrong. The sex had been magnificent. Spectacular. But now I was terrified because I knew I'd just become another of the many women he had on rotation in his bed night after night.

And this bothered me a great deal because I'd known exactly what I was getting myself into.

Dumb.

But I wasn't going to go into this blind so I blurted, "What happens now?"

I tensed up when I heard him sigh. "Well, we close our eyes then this thing called sleep overtakes us. It's a normal condition where the body…"

I snorted softly. "You know what I mean, Ryker."

He moved back a bit and looked down at me. I could only see the outline of his face but knew he probably had that damned smirk on his face.

"I'd like to hook up with you again, Francesca. That what you mean?"

I swallowed roughly, knowing exactly what he was saying which, of course, hadn't been what I'd meant at all. And now my feelings were hurt because even though it was ridiculous, I desperately wanted him to want me as much as I wanted him but I saw that just wasn't going to happen.

So I nodded then he folded himself around me holding me tightly.

For me, my entire world had changed.

For him, he'd added another notch to his bedpost.

6—Face Off

I left Ryker's in the middle of the night after we'd gone another delicious but heartbreaking round since I knew it was the last time I'd be with him. Afterward, he'd enclosed me in his arms, kissed me sweetly and drifted off. I'd waited until I was sure he was asleep before slipping out of his hold.

I thanked the Almighty that Sharee wasn't awake when I got home and after getting into bed, I lay there staring at my ceiling for an ungodly amount of time, my stomach twisted in knots at knowing Ryker and I were finished.

I figured I could talk to Sharee and Gladys about it to see if I had other alternatives, but I knew Ree would only say, "You're getting laid. Go with it," and Gladys would probably tell me to enjoy it while it lasted, which were both basically the same thing. I wondered if I *could* do that, just sleep with Ryker not expecting anything to come from it then move on when it ended, but decided there was no way that would work for me. I was a relationship type of gal, a one-man woman, and knowing he was sleeping with other women was a huge turnoff and something I wouldn't do.

Besides, I liked him way too much and knew I'd only hurt worse if I continued seeing him.

I choked out a soft sob deciding I had to be finished with it all. I felt I deserved so much more and if Ryker Powers couldn't give me what I wanted, I had no choice but to move on. So once again I was faced with a more than bleak romantic future when I realized he wouldn't be part of it.

And that hurt my heart.

~*~*~*~

The next morning I got up in a better mood than what I thought I would, excited for my second day of coaching. I dressed in jeans and the Montlake Elementary t-shirt and zippered hoodie Coach Gilbert had given me yesterday, smiling as I laced up my tennis shoes because I couldn't wait to get in there and have some fun with the kids. Maybe we'd get out the parachute today if Coach G approved, but knowing him he'd probably make us use it as a life net to catch kids while he had them jump from the bleacher tops.

I felt even better when my first class came in and I chuckled at all the smiling faces.

"Hi, Coach Man-ja-jelly!" the first graders cried which had me cracking up at their mispronunciation of my last name.

"It's pronounced Man-ja-nell-ee," I heard a deep voice say and I spun to see Ryker standing there with a shit-eating grin on his face.

What the hell was he doing here? And be still my heart because he looked so damned good. Shit!

"Surprise," he said, still grinning then spun a basketball on his pointer finger making the kids race over to where he was to give him their oohhs and aahhs.

Shit again.

I turned back to Coach G when he shouted, "Give me five laps!" then watched as the little ones took off, some colliding with each other while others complained loudly to Coach G that kids were cutting corners of the gym floor.

"You just happy to see me or is that a whistle in your pocket?" Ryker said from behind.

I'm sure I don't have to describe the look on my face as I turned to face him.

"What're you doing here?" I asked with a scowl.

He shrugged. "It's where I was assigned."

"But you weren't here yesterday!"

"Had a meet."

Oh, yeah. Double shit.

I walked over to Coach G who was drinking coffee from a travel mug in the middle of the gym floor watching the kids run. "Coach? Um, I thought maybe we could get the parachute out?"

"Sorry, kid. Ryker here wants to play some basketball. We've already set up the six-foot goals."

I glared back at Ryker whose mouth twitched at the corner. Ass.

"Oh, okay. You know, I played basketball at Hallervan. I'm sure I can show them a few things."

"I'd like to see your moves," Ryker mumbled from behind me as the kids came running over.

"Coach Powers! Are we playing basketball? Cool!" the kids said as they circled around him.

"Yep. Let's get you divided into teams," Ryker said proceeding to take charge of everything.

Jerk.

It was decided that I'd coach one team and Ryker would take the other, and, oh, I was going to beat his ass, but with one minute left, Ryker's team scored a basket to tie the score.

"Why don't you two get in there and play? Help them out a little," Coach G hollered.

A timeout was called and I made the adjustments.

"Okay, everyone stay with the man you were guarding," I instructed.

A little girl named Ella raised her hand. "But there aren't any men out there."

I chuckled. "That's just what you call the person you're guarding," I explained.

"What's guarding?" Jason inquired.

"It's staying on the man—er, person, you're assigned to and keeping them from scoring."

"Oh!" he said. "I can do that!"

"Good. So here's what we're gonna do. Jennifer, you're the best shooter so when I bring the ball down, you go stand right by the basket. Aaron, you get on the free throw line." I described as clearly as I could what I wanted them to do and they all nodded their heads when I asked if they understood. "Okay, let's break!"

We all put our hands in then said, "Go, Geckos!" which was the name they'd come up with for our team.

I had Zach take the ball out and throw to me and I dribbled it up the court where I was met with Ryker who was guarding me. I dribbled right up to him making it look like he could get the ball, but when he swiped at it, I did a between the legs dribble to switch directions sweeping right by him and took off right down the middle of the court to the basket. My team had surprisingly set up just the way I'd told them and when I got to the middle of the lane, I bounce passed to Jennifer for her to take the shot. But I never got to see it.

Ryker came in right behind me, and trying to knock the ball out of my hands he missed and ended up running smack dab into me and we both went flying. Luckily, he grabbed me around the waist and twisted us in midair to where when we landed I landed with my back to his front. We both landed with an OOMPH!

As I lay there in shock at what just happened, gasping for air, I felt him shaking with laughter underneath me.

"Seem to recall being in this same position with you last night," he muttered, wrapping his arms tighter around me.

"Let me go!" I hissed elbowing him in the ribs hard enough to make him grunt. Good. He let me go and I scrambled up quickly, turning to glare down at him as I smoothed out my mussed hair and jacket. He stood up slowly, a wicked smile on his face and then the questions began.

"Are you okay, Miss Coach Manjajelly?"

"Do you need to go to the nurse's office? I know where it is! I go every day!"

"I'm okay! No, I don't need to go see the nurse!"

"Coach Powers, you hurted her!" said one little girl who was tugging on his hoodie.

He squatted down in front of her. "I think Coach Mangenelli will be fine. But if you think I should, I can kiss her booboos all better later."

"Yay! You *should* kiss her booboos! She'll feel a lot better after that! My mommy always kisses my booboos and they don't hurt no more!"

"Okay, Bridget, I'll definitely do that," he agreed giving me not only a smirk but a wink as Bridget danced around him singing a song about booboos not hurting anymore.

Lord.

"Coach?" Jennifer, my little shooter said quietly.

I looked down at her and asked, "Yes?"

She gazed shyly up at me shuffling her feet around. "I made the shot so we won."

My smile was so big it hurt my face. "Thatta girl!" I picked her up and spun her around as she giggled then gave her a high five after putting her down.

"All right. Time to head back to class! Line up!" Coach G called gruffly and I watched as twenty-two first graders immediately obeyed getting into their respective lines fairly quickly (and neatly, I might add). "Tomorrow's Friday so it's free day. You can play whatever you want."

Twenty-two little voices cried out, "Dodge ball!" which amazed me that they'd choose to come back for more of the grueling game.

"We'll decide tomorrow," Coach G declared.

"Thanks, Coach Gilbert," their teacher who'd shown up called with a wave.

Arms across his chest, Coach G nodded at her then looked first at Ryker then me. "I need coffee. Fifth graders'll be coming in in about five. I'm not back, get 'em started with something." I watched as he followed the class out then turned to see Ryker adjusting the goals to eight feet.

"What're you doing?" I asked.

"Getting ready for the next class," he explained.

"No. I mean, what are you *doing*?"

He glanced at me then turned back to his task. "Told you already."

I knew my ego was talking as I surmised he must've seen where I was doing my teaching and had put in a request for it even though it was highly unlikely that would happen. I still wouldn't have put it past the fact that he could've charmed some giddy professor into placing him here.

"Just so you know, I'm finished with you," I mumbled as I bent to pick up a basketball. When I stood and turned to him, I gasped because he was right there all up in my space.

"Are you now?" he asked looking down at me, his expression and tone bordering on dangerous. He took a step forward making me back up against the wall. "You weren't finished with me last night after I made you come so hard you couldn't even move."

I pushed off on his chest with the basketball I was holding, getting away from him. "That's all you ever think about, isn't it? Just because you can give me amazing orgasms doesn't mean we have something. You even said it yourself. All you want from me is another hookup, right?"

He stared at me with narrowed eyes. "What do you want from me, Francesca? We've fucked twice. You expecting me to propose?"

Was he serious right now?

"No!" I hissed. God, he was such a jerk. "I don't want anything from you."

"Hey, Coach Mangenelli!" a couple of the fifth graders who were coming in called.

"Hey, guys!" I answered, ignoring the fact that I'd allowed my heart to break once again at the hands of Ryker Powers.

~*~*~*~

I didn't say another word to Ryker as the day went on. It wasn't that I was ignoring him; there just wasn't a reason for me to chat him up. When Coach G came back from his coffee break, we jumped right back into the routine with the other classes, Ryker and I coaching against each other (without incident but at least my teams won again) before he left at lunch to go to wrestling practice.

When I got home Sharee was on her phone FaceTiming with Gladys.

"So you didn't come home last night, you whore!" Gladys accused.

God.

I cut my eyes at Sharee before announcing, "Yes, I'm a whore. A huge one. But that's all over now."

"Why?" they said in unison.

Letting out a sigh, I sat on the couch next to Sharee. "He doesn't want a relationship. He just wants to hook up. I want more. It's over." Gladys started to say something and I interrupted. "Before you both tell me to enjoy being laid before moving on, you know I can't do that. I'm just not made that way."

"But he was good, right?" Gladys inquired.

Another sigh. "The best."

I thought their silence at the demise of my dream was generous until Gladys started talking.

"You need to make him jealous."

I rolled my eyes. "You can't make someone jealous who doesn't want you, Glad."

"But you can try!" she said with a giggle.

"No, I'm not gonna try to make him jealous. I'm just gonna move on and everything will work out the way it's supposed to. Or at least that's what Mrs. Bertolini told me this morning when I was sneaking in. Since when does she go out on her balcony at four in the morning? She scared the shit out of me when she whispered 'Gotcha!'"

"She's psychic," Sharee muttered. "She knew you'd be coming home."

"I'm beginning to think she is," Gladys whispered reverently.

"Anyway," I began, rolling my eyes at both of them, "I'm starting over."

"Good idea!" Gladys agreed which made me snort since she'd just been the one telling me to make Ryker jealous.

"Party Saturday. Wish you could be here," Sharee told Gladys.

Gladys' pouty face filled the screen. "Me too. But, ooooh! Perfect opportunity for you to meet someone, Frankie! Then rub that shit in that Ryker guy's face!"

"Told you I'm not doing that. And, oh, yay! Another party! Like the last one didn't land me in a shit ton of trouble." I gave Sharee a look. "I'm not going."

"Oh, yes, you are," she informed me. "SAE's are having their annual Welcome Back to Hell party and it's huge. Everyone who's anyone will be there."

"Guess I'm not anyone," I declared.

"Yes, you are! And you have to go!" Gladys begged.

I frowned. "Why's it so important that I go?"

"Because… because you're a senior and you're gonna graduate soon and be an adult and not have time to party anymore. That's why!" Gladys shared.

"We'll see. Well, I've gotta run to Mom and Dad's for dinner." I looked at Sharee. "You sure you can't come?"

She shook her head. "I've got class."

"Mom's gonna be disappointed but she'll deal, I guess," I told her. "Love you, Glad!" I said to the phone, kissing my fingers and putting them to the screen then got off the couch and went to my bedroom to change.

After coming out of my bedroom and hollering goodbye, I headed to the front door and heard Gladys telling Sharee that it was sad that my dreams had been destroyed.

"It doesn't mean my life is over just because some guy and I didn't work out!" I hollered through gritted teeth. "I'm gonna be fine."

I knew they were only concerned for me, but I couldn't help slamming the door just a little before I left.

"How's my baby girl?" Dad asked as he wrapped his arms around me when I came in.

"I'm good, Daddy," I returned when he let me go and took my coat.

"How's teaching?" Mom called from the kitchen.

"It's good too," I called back then went toward the kitchen to help her with dinner.

"Get the bread out of the oven, would you?" Mom instructed after giving me a kiss on the cheek when I came in.

Dad had followed me and now leaned against the counter. "So you're teaching PE, huh?"

"*Coaching*, Daddy," I answered as I put an oven mitt on. "I'm Coach Manjajelly," I said with a snort as I bent to pull the garlic bread out.

"Oh, coaching. I see," he said with a chuckle. Dad had hoped I'd go into engineering, following in his footsteps, but I'd explained to him that teaching was a calling, almost like preaching, I guessed, and it's what I felt I was supposed to do. He still balked a little at my career choice but he was beginning to come around.

"Coach Manjajelly?" Mom questioned as she put pasta on our plates.

"The first graders can't seem to say my last name." I set the bread on the stovetop.

"Why don't you tell them to call you Frankie?" Dad asked as he carried the plates to the table.

"Tony. She can't have her students calling her by her first name," Mom scolded.

"Coach M, then," he answered with a shrug.

"That works," I muttered as I put a cloth in a basket then tossed the hot slices of bread into it.

"Come on," Mom prompted. "It's ready." She carried the pot of sauce to the table and told me to grab the salad bowl on my way in.

We chatted a bit while Dad poured our wine and we put salad in our bowls and sauce onto our noodles. Then it got really fun.

"Sharee says you met a boy," Mom declared.

Holy shit. I was going to kill her. Class or not, no wonder she didn't want to come with me tonight.

"Uh, well, yeah, I guess I did," I mumbled.

"Who is he?" Dad asked.

"Just some guy."

"Sharee said his name's Ryker and he's a wrestler and very handsome!" Mom cooed.

Great.

"He's nice looking," I supplied with a scowl. Sharee was getting her ass kicked when she got home tonight.

"So are you dating?" Mom asked, twirling noodles around her fork and looking at me almost rabidly.

Good grief. Mom's twin sister Valerie's daughter, my cousin Gia, had just had a baby and now Mom was dying to be a grandma.

"Vi," Dad warned.

"What? I'm asking my only child if she's dating someone. What's wrong with that?"

Dad shook his head and kept eating.

"We're not dating, Mom," I explained.

"Why not?"

I sighed. "Because he's not interested. We're just, uh, friends."

The look of disappointment on her face killed but whatever. I was only twenty-two. There was still plenty of time for me to give her the gazillion grandkids that she craved.

"Why wouldn't he be interested? Look at you! You're beautiful, intelligent, sweet! The boy must be out of his mind! And what kind of name is Ryker?"

"Vi."

"What, Anthony?" Oh, lord. She was calling him by his full name which meant she was pissed.

"Mom, he's just not into relationships."

"What do you mean not into relationships? Sharee said you spent the night with him!"

Bad time to be taking a drink of wine.

"I'm gonna kill her," I choked out, wiping my mouth on my napkin.

"Topic change," Dad insisted. "How about those Mariners? Huh?"

I wanted to laugh and cry at the same time. Sharee, Gladys and I always joked about how when Dad was uncomfortable with a conversation, he'd bring up the Mariners. But right now I was immeasurably glad I kept up with the local sports teams because he and I launched into a conversation about baseball while Mom pouted. Jesus.

After dinner, I helped clear the table and did the dishes keeping up the sports chat with Dad so Mom couldn't ask about Ryker again.

"So have you met any other boys?" Mom's curiosity got the better of her when I started the dishwasher.

"No, not really. Don't worry, though. I'm sure I'll find one and be knocked up before you know it. The playing field between you and Aunt Val will be even in no time." I couldn't help but be a little annoyed by this point.

"Frankie!" she chided.

I turned to her. "Well, that's what you want, right?"

"Yes, but you don't have to be crass about it."

I rolled my eyes but felt bad that I'd been rude. "Sorry. It's just a touchy topic right now."

"Why?"

"Let it go, Vi. Can't you see she doesn't want to talk about it?"

Thank you, Dad!

Before Mom could keep going, I said, "I'm gonna head back. I've got classes tomorrow, so I need to get some sleep. Thank you for dinner." I gave them each a hug and kiss promising to come back next week.

Sitting in my car before taking off, I texted Sharee.

Text Message—Thurs, Jan 15, 9:23 p.m.

Me: Just warning you I hate you very much right now

Text Message—Thurs, Jan 15, 9:23 p.m.

Ree: LOL

Text Message—Thurs, Jan 15, 9:23 p.m.

Me: You'll think LOL when I get home

Text Message—Thurs, Jan 15, 9:24 p.m.

Ree: You should call your mom more often so she doesn't have to call me to find out what's going on in her only child's life. The woman should've been a detective with her powers of persuasion at making me talk. Sorry.

By the time I got home Sharee was gone, having texted a few minutes before I got there saying she had to run to get shampoo which was a good thing because I was in a mood and a half. But I was tired, so after showering and putting on my pjs, I plopped into bed and was out like a light, not even hearing her come in.

~*~*~*~

Ryker wasn't at school the next day. Coach G informed me that he had a tournament out of town, which I told myself I couldn't have cared less. My classes went great with all of them opting to play dodgeball which still made me shake my head, and this time only a total of eight kids had to go to the nurse's office all day, which Coach G said was an all-time low.

By the end of the day I was beat, having jumped in to play a bit with the kids because I must've been out of my freaking mind. The younger grades weren't bad but some of the older kids weren't lacking in ball-throwing skills making me duck, dive and dodge to avoid being knocked upside the head several times. Jeez. I couldn't wait to get home and have a long soak in the tub but when I got there Sharee told me I needed to go somewhere with her.

"But I don't wanna," I whined like one of my first graders throwing myself onto the sofa.

"It'll be fun," Sharee assured me.

"I feel like I'm eighty."

"Whatever. Get your octogenarian ass in the shower and get ready."

"Where're we going?" I moaned.

"It's a surprise."

Pulling myself up off the couch and giving Sharee a grouchy look, I limped to my bedroom to get some clothes then hobbled out and down to the bathroom. God, I was only twenty-two. I needed to start working out again. Yay.

"Okay, I'm ready," I called from my room.

"Let's go!"

I had to catch up with her outside as she jumped into her Saab.

"Good grief. What's going on?" I asked buckling my seatbelt.

"You'll see!" she semi-squealed. I knew it had to be something big because Sharee rarely squealed about anything.

When we ended up at the airport, I asked with a frown, "What're we doing here?"

"C'mon!" she said, getting out of the car.

I followed her into the airport to concourse C wondering what the heck was going on until we made it around the corner and I heard someone screaming.

"What the..." I barely got out before being tackle hugged.

The next thing I knew, Sharee, Gladys and I were jumping up and down in a group hug.

"What are you doing here?" I finally asked, astonished that she'd flown in.

"I left some stuff at Mom and Dad's over Christmas and they couldn't send it all to me, so I'm back to get it! I wasn't sure when I could make it until Ree told me about the party tomorrow night, and I thought it'd be perfect for me to come so we could help find you a new boyfriend!"

Oh, my God. Talk about spoiling the fun.

I gave both of them a disgusted look. "I don't need a boyfriend."

"We'll talk about that later. Let's get out of here!" Gladys suggested, picking up the carry-on she'd dropped to hug Sharee and me, then looping her arm through mine she pulled me back through the airport with her.

In the car on the way to the apartment, Gladys showed us pictures of her latest designs, and we all three screamed when she told us that Michael Kors had come by to give a lecture. I was so glad she was happy and loving what she was doing.

"Before we go to your apartment, my lovely friends, take a detour! I'm taking you to Spinasse!" She turned and looked back at me. "I owe you, remember?"

I remembered all right. And I was definitely going to let her buy me dinner, if not only for the fact that her parents were both doctors and had money coming out the wazoo and she could afford it, but she'd promised anyway.

"Sounds great!" Sharee said as she took the exit that would get us to the restaurant.

"And when we're there, we'll figure out what kinda guy we need to find for you," Gladys tacked on.

I huffed. "Why am I the charity case all of a sudden? Ree's single too. And so are you for that matter!"

Gladys chuckled. "Oh, I've got my eye on someone and Ree just got out of a relationship. You're the only one who needs someone!"

"Seriously? I don't *need* anyone, Glad. Can't we just have fun hanging out while you're here?" I saw her glance at Sharee who shrugged. "I mean it! If I'm supposed to be with someone, I'll be with them. Leave it alone. Please!"

Here's the deal. The reason I was so irritated (other than the fact that they wouldn't leave things alone) was they'd done this to me a couple times before, ganged up on me in a way. At the end of our sophomore year in high school, my first year there, they'd decided I needed to run for Miss Greenling. Since I was new, I had no idea about the pageant title but I'd done pageants in Texas when I was little so I was okay with the idea. Until I figured out what *Greenling* meant when I'd won and was made to pose for pictures holding a stinky, slimy *fish* acting as if I was kissing it. It'd taken me a couple days to get over being mad at them, neither having understood my embarrassment since they'd known what the pageant was about and that was the normal thing the winner did.

Then there was the Chris Swartz incident our junior year when they'd made it very clear to him that I had a crush on him at which he'd just snorted and the very next day had very demonstratively come out of the closet by holding Tommy Kinzer's hand in the hallway.

"We're just trying to help," Sharee mumbled.

"I know, but I don't need your help," I mumbled right back.

We were quiet for a few minutes before pulling into Spinasse and Gladys broke the silence. "Okay. We'll let it drop. But only if you promise to have a look around tomorrow night. Deal?" She and Sharee turned to look at me.

Good lord. I needed to get new friends.

"Whatever," I answered with a roll of my eyes and got out of the car.

~*~*~*~

It was Saturday night and we were getting ready for the SAE party, which I couldn't *not* go to since Gladys was here. I just hoped she and Sharee cooled it on trying to hook me up with someone.

"Here! Wear this!" Gladys said, coming into my bathroom holding up a gorgeous cream-colored, long-sleeved lacy blouse. "I made it last week. Isn't it adorable?"

"It's beautiful. You sure?" I asked, pushing off the counter where I'd been leaning to put on my mascara in the mirror.

"Yes! I made it with you in mind so it's yours! That color will go perfectly with your olive skin!" She looked at me for a second then at the shirt for another, finger on her bottom lip before saying, "It needs something." She hung the shirt on the shower curtain rod and stared at it for a moment more before the light bulb went on over her head and she scurried out of the bathroom. When she came back in she held a gorgeous black silk scarf with pink flowers on it. "This is what it needs," she stated as she draped it around the neckline of the blouse. "Keep this too."

"Wow," I remarked in awe as I looked at it. It looked perfect. "How do you know this stuff?" I asked.

"I don't know. I think it's kinda like a cook who knows which spice to put in." She shrugged. "And let's hope this Ryker guy's there and sees you in this, so when you find a new boyfriend, he'll be really jealous."

Here we went again.

I took a deep breath, trying to control my temper, so tired of hearing that. "He won't be there. He's at a tournament out of town." Gladys raised an eyebrow at me in the mirror while she smoothed on some lip gloss. "Coach G told me yesterday in PE why he was gone. That's the only reason I know." I shrugged nonchalantly letting her know I couldn't have cared less but I'm sure I didn't fool her.

"Darn. I wanted him to be there so you could show him what he's missing out on when we find you someone else."

Okay, I'd had it.

"I've had it!" I shrieked. "Stop trying to set me up! Jesus!" Sharee walked into the bathroom just then and did a turnabout. "Oh no. You get your ass back in here!" I called. When she reluctantly came back, I continued. "Both of you stop it. I know you love me and that's why you're doing this ganging up thing again but stop." Their looks of innocence first at me then at each other made me want to smack them. "Greenling? Chris Swartz? Remember?" At least they both nodded knowing what I was getting at which made me calm down. "Look. I'm fine. I don't need anyone. If I find someone, well, whoopee for me. But if not, I'm good. So for the last time, get it through your thick skulls that I'm fine, okay?"

They both nodded again.

Gladys and I continued our makeup routine in silence until Sharee broke it. "How 'bout those Mariners?"

We all burst into laughter and the conversation was behind us. Thank God.

And even though they dropped it, I still secretly hoped I'd find someone. I mean, not at this party just somewhere. Because although I tried acting like I didn't care about Ryker I knew I still did, which sucked. But I also knew I needed to move on.

And that's what I planned on doing.

I had to admit the party was kind of fun. It was nice to be out with my girls again. And right now I was talking to a really cute guy named Cole who was a wrestler. What was it with me and wrestlers? Yeesh. Anyway, he'd found us a cozy corner where we could talk, and let me say he was pretty easy on the eyes. He was handsome, tall and freaking built. His blond hair was longish, meeting his square jaw and his sky blue eyes were rimmed by dark lashes. What wasn't to like? Sadly, though, I couldn't help thinking that I preferred dark hair and golden eyes that glimmered with mischief. Damn it.

"So, why aren't you at the tournament?" I asked before taking a sip of my drink.

"I had to redshirt this year because of a preseason shoulder injury. Coach has had me stay home when we travel because it wouldn't do any good for me to go." He shrugged.

"You'd probably get bored, huh?"

He gave me a million-dollar smile. "Bored as fuck. I'd probably end up just getting into trouble trying to talk to pretty girls like you." He winked and I swear I swooned like an idiot. I couldn't help it. He was hot.

Just not as hot as someone else I knew but I reminded myself that I was moving on, so I put that thought out of my head.

I learned that Cole was from Oregon and had been an All-American wrestler for Hallervan his last two years here. He liked that I'd played basketball and had been an All-American too, saying that our kids would be "hella athletes" which at any other time I'd have been thrilled to hear a guy saying that. Just not right now. When he told me he was a business major and wanted to own his own oil supply company someday, I knew Dad would love him.

"Hey, I've gotta go see a man about a horse," he said with another gorgeous smile. "I'll be back with fresh drinks." He leaned down and brushed his lips against mine surprising the hell out of me. "Beautiful," he murmured before winking again and going to do his business.

"Oh, wow! He's ca-yute!" Gladys shrieked as she bounced up to me. She was already three sheets to the wind, having had at least two glasses of wine, the lightweight.

"He is cute," I agreed, sniffing first then sipping whatever concoction was in the red cup she'd handed me. It wasn't bad, so I slipped that cup inside my empty one deciding to keep it.

"Oh, but *that* guy? He's *really* cute!" she said, pointing at a guy in jeans and a maroon Hallervan t-shirt who was standing in a group across the room to my right. "I'm gonna go find out what his name is! Then I'll bring him back and introduce him to you!"

"I'm doing just fine on my own," I said but she was already gone. Good God. I shook my head as I watched her push her way through the crowd.

While I focused on her talking to the guy she'd pointed out, I canted my head to the side thinking he looked familiar, I just didn't know from where. And when she grabbed his upper arm and started dragging him toward me, I contemplated running. We'd taken a cab here so I figured it'd take me at least six seconds to make it to the front door—I had on five-inch heels and there was a crowd. If she gave chase, I knew I'd have to get at least fifty yards from the frat house before she'd give up since Gladys didn't do running—another thirty seconds or so. Then I'd call for a cab—who knew how long it'd take to get here but if this kept me from being tracked down by her to face certain embarrassment, who cared. And then I'd be in the clear.

So let's see, face Gladys trying to force this poor guy on me, being humiliated to no end as she explained to him that my would-be soulmate had only wanted me for a couple booty calls, *or* undoubtedly spraining an ankle (or both) running away, possibly falling and scraping a knee (or both) in the process and maybe tearing my favorite pair of jeans.

I saw her yanking on his arm harder and getting closer.

Decision made.

I set my cups down and just as I spun to go, she exclaimed, "Frankie! Look who it is!"

Shit. So close.

I turned back with a grimace to see her hanging all over a smaller, leaner version of Ryker.

What the hell?

"Uh..." I began not knowing what to say.

"This is Loch! Isn't he *adorable*?" she squealed, taking his chin in her fingers and squeezing while she shook his head.

Why, lord? What had I ever done to deserve this?

"Hey," the guy said with a grin and holding out his hand. "I'm Loch Powers."

Oh fuck.

Fuck!

"H-Hey, Loch," I returned, reaching out to shake his hand trying not to freak out. "Frankie Mangenelli." I next looked at Gladys and instructed, "You can take your hand off his face now."

At hearing my name, he jerked his head back and narrowed his eyes at me as if in recognition. "Frankie?"

"Oh! Sorry!" Gladys interrupted with a giggle letting his chin go then patting his sculpted chest and giving his pec a squeeze. Good lord.

She giggled again but something else caught her attention. "Oh, my gosh! I think that's Ashley Weathers over there! Be right back!" she said in her sing-songy Gladys way and took off, flitting through the crowd.

I looked back at Loch. "Sorry about that. She's a bit drunk, not that there's any difference between when she's sober. And, yes, Frankie."

The famous Powers smirk graced his beautiful face. "I know who you are."

I frowned. "You do?"

"I do," he said with a chuckle.

We stood staring at each other for a moment before I finally prompted through my own narrowed eyes, "Care to fill me in?"

"You've gone out with my older brother Ryker."

My eyes got huge then. Had Ryker talked about me? Surely not. No way Mr. Hookup would divulge his interest in one woman and damage his player reputation, even to his own brother. "Oh, um, yeah, I did."

"He must really like you…"

This made me frown again. "Why do you say that?"

"Well, Ryker's, uh, kinda… popular… with, um, women." Loch actually had the decency to look uncomfortable upon letting *that* clearly conspicuous cat out of the bag.

His proclamation made me feel *so* much better about having stuck around. I nodded knowingly several times before announcing, "Well, it was nice meeting you, Loch." I gave him a forced smile and turned to leave, putting Operation Blow This Joint into action when he grabbed my hand keeping me from leaving. I looked back at him, eyebrow raised.

"That didn't come out right, Frankie," he explained. "What I'm trying to tell you is that Ryker isn't a big sharer."

As I waited for him to explain this cryptic remark, Sharee came walking up. Oh yay.

"Who's this, Frankie?" she questioned with a grin, nodding at Loch.

"This is—"

"Loch Powers," he interrupted, holding out his hand to her which she took while giving me a smirk.

"Loch Powers. Any relation to Ryker?" she inquired.

"He's my older brother."

She now gave me a smart look and I rolled my eyes. "Oh, cool! You know Frankie here has gone out with your brother?"

"I do."

He grinned at me and I was back to getting the hell out of there when Cole walked up, handing me a fresh drink. And this night just kept getting better. Loch was going to think I was the whore that I obviously was who now was hitting on yet another wrestler.

"What's up, Cole?" Loch asked.

"Hey, Loch. Just living the dream," Cole replied with a grin. "You hear how they did?"

Loch started in on some wrestling speak that I didn't understand and I gave Sharee a warning look which only made her chuckle. Oh, how I loved my friends. She sidled over next to me and bumped my shoulder with hers.

"What?" I snapped under my breath.

"Looks like you're doing okay for yourself tonight. Cole's cute."

I looked at him as I leaned over to whisper to her. "He is cute. Nice too. I'm ready to leave."

She laughed and threw an arm around my shoulders. "Nah. It's just getting good." I shook my head and tuned in to what the guys were saying to hear Loch say, "An hour ago," whatever that meant.

"Cool," Cole commented then looked at me. "You wanna go somewhere quiet so we can talk?"

Sharee nudged me with her elbow which annoyed the hell out of me. "Sure. We can go back to our little corner if you'd like," I answered.

Disappointment passed over Cole's face but whatever. No way was I going to leave with him because first of all, although extremely cute, I knew I wasn't into him, and secondly, I didn't want Loch to know beyond the shadow of a doubt that I was some kind of hooker. Nope. I wanted it remain a mystery. Ergh.

"Nice meeting you, Loch," I said over my shoulder as Cole took my hand so we could retreat to our earlier space.

Once there, Cole still held my hand and announced, "I like you, Frankie," as he gazed into my eyes.

Well, wasn't I just the likeable one lately?

With a cringe I answered, "Thanks," not knowing how else to respond.

You'd think I'd have had everything in my head absolutely figured out by now, but as I bit my lip it came to me that I was still hooked on Ryker and it was going to take time to get over him. Ding ding ding! Revelation!

Cole snorted at my response and I guess I must've been giving mixed signals because he leaned in to give me a kiss which I dodged by putting my hand to his chest. His very hard, muscular chest. Damn.

"I'm sorry. I need to let you know that—" and that's when I felt eyes on me. I shivered as my eyes drifted down from his face past his left shoulder to scan the room but I saw nothing. Weird.

At my look of consternation, Cole asked, "You okay?" He glanced over his shoulder to see what I'd been looking at turning back to me in question.

"Yes, I'm fine. Someone just walked across my grave, I guess." I chuckled at his confused expression. "My upstairs neighbor says that. Guess she's rubbing off on me." I looked down at my drink and shook my head in embarrassment when I heard a deep voice from behind Cole which made my body go rigid.

I looked up as Ryker asked, "Having a good time, Francesca?" His amber eyes shone in amusement as he lifted a brow.

Oh hell.

"Hey, Ryke. How'd you do?" Cole said.

Keeping his eyes on me, Ryker stated, "Advanced through all three rounds. Picked up a fall in the second for two points. Won the fourth by technical fall."

"Damn. That's fuckin' badass. Congrats, man," Cole uttered sounding like he was very impressed.

I was impressed too but mostly because Ryker had won, not because I knew a damned thing about wrestling. Since basketball and wrestling shared the same season, I'd never really gotten to watch it or learn the terminology. But from the way Cole was acting, it was apparent Ryker had done very well.

"Thanks," Ryker muttered still not moving his eyes away from me. Gah.

"You two know each other?" Cole looked suspiciously between us.

I bit my lip and fidgeted with my cup a little as Ryker stared me down before answering. "We might've broken a bed spring or two a couple times."

My head shot up and I blinked at him with my mouth hanging open.

What?

What!

Oh. My. God.

I gasped as I looked up at him shocked at what he'd said, only to see him smirking back at me.

Holy fucking shit.

Cole's face looked confused then he chuckled. "You what?"

"I-I've gotta go," I stammered.

I was pissed and flustered and boiling mad and needed to get the hell out of there before I started wailing on Ryker right then and there for once again screwing with my head. I handed Cole my cup giving him a small smile mixed with a look of apology, shaking my head at him before taking off to find Sharee and Gladys.

Making my way through the crowd, I sensed Ryker following me, the asshole, but I kept going. As far as I was concerned, he could follow me to the ends of the earth and I still wouldn't fucking stop for him. Bastard. He'd made it clear what he wanted from me and he did *not* get to go around making me look bad or ruining potential dates I may or may not have gone on. When I got to the kitchen and didn't see either of my friends, I looped around through the crowd toward the front door deciding I'd just have to text them and let them know I'd left.

I'd just made it out the door and was heading down the steps when Ryker barked out, "Stop, Francesca!"

"Fuck you, Ryker," I fired back, not turning to look at him as I took a right at the bottom of the steps keeping the same pace as I pulled my phone from my back pocket to call for a taxi. Of course there were people everywhere who heard our exchange and some guy snorted at the spectacle I'm sure we were making.

"Goddamn it," I heard Ryker hiss from right behind me just before he grabbed my arm spinning me to face him.

"Get your hands off me," I bit out, flinging my arm out of his grip as I glowered up at him. Just looking at him made me want to punch him, and I knew I needed to take off again because I didn't feel like going to jail for assault and battery tonight. I put my phone back in my pocket deciding the call could wait, my main goal for now being to get as far away from this prick as possible.

Just as I tried getting away, he stepped right in my path blocking me, his eyes sparking with anger. "I told you to stop."

What the hell was he mad about? He was the asshole who basically told Cole I'd slept with him. I was the one who should be mad.

"I don't give a fuck what you told me," I spit out.

We were at the side of the frat house now and if I wasn't as angry as I was, I'd have found his appearance a little daunting, the shadows of the trees on his face giving him a sinister air. But I was fuming and didn't really give a rip at the moment.

"Watch that dirty mouth of yours, Francesca," he warned taking a few steps forward, backing me against the house, his eyes practically glowing.

Oh, *I* was the one with the dirty mouth now. I huffed out a pissed off laugh. "Or what? You're gonna fucking spank me again?"

His hand slid up over the scarf to grip me around the throat, not threateningly but firmly, then he leaned in and growled in my ear, "Or I'll put something in it to shut you up."

For the second time tonight I found myself shoving my hands against rock-hard pecs. Jeez.

"Get away from me!" I bit out.

Ryker dropped his hand from my neck and stepped back a little, his eyes still intense on mine.

"Who do you think you are, huh?" I snapped. "Are you trying to make me look like a tramp? Because, let me tell you, I'm doing a fine job of it on my own and I *don't need your help*!" I emphasized the last part because it was the damned truth. I stood there breathing hard as I glared up at him, the breath emanating from my mouth in white puffs with each exhalation. I'd forgotten to grab my coat and now ran my hands up and down my arms for warmth while stating, "You tell me you only want a 'hookup' but when you see me talking to someone else you screw any chance of my getting with him by telling him we've slept together? What *is* that?"

As I was speaking, I watched him unzipping his hoodie and taking it off. When his arms went around me I flinched thinking he was going to "trap" me again until I realized he'd draped his jacket over my shoulders to keep me warm. Ugh. Now I couldn't even be as mad at him as I wanted to be.

I crossed my arms and gripped the sides of the hoodie and unable to help myself tilted my head down to my right shoulder and closing my eyes took a surreptitious whiff finding that it smelled just like him, all clean with a hint of a warm spice. Ugh.

Drive that knife in deeper, Frankie. Smash those last pieces of your heart into dust.

"What do you want from me?" I whispered looking up at him.

He shook his head before muttering, "I don't know."

Well, at least he was being up front about it. Even though I'd have loved for him to tell me that what he wanted from me was *me*, he couldn't live without me and he wanted to be with me forever, I knew that was just the dreamer in me. Man, this dreamer persona seriously needed to take a freaking hike.

I stared at him for several seconds before eventually speaking. "Thank you for being honest." I saw his mouth curl up at the sides probably at my sudden mood change. "I get it now," I shared as I nodded. "But since we're not gonna be together, you really can't be doing things like you did earlier. I mean, what if I'd wanted to go out with Cole?"

His eyes flared (what was that about?) then he decreed, "He's not someone you should go out with."

I rolled my eyes at his big brother demeanor. "And why's that? From what I saw, he's a nice guy."

"Not so sure the mother of his son would agree."

My brow came down. "What?"

"He's got a kid. Born right before season started. Cole tells us all he's gonna marry this chick then he goes and fucks everything in sight."

"Oh." Crap.

Ryker kept his eyes on mine before they moved down to my lips for a moment before he gave what I thought was a frustrated sigh. He next rubbed his hands over his face and asked, "You need a ride?"

"I was gonna get a cab."

"Come on." He grabbed my hand and started walking up the street pulling me along with him. When we got to an orange sixty-something Mustang, he said, "Here," and taking the hoodie from my shoulders helped me put my arms into it and zipped me up, the whole time looking like he wanted to say something but keeping quiet. After opening the passenger door he put his hand at the small of my back and guided me inside and I watched him walk distractedly to the driver's side, running his hand through his hair as he did. When he got in, he started the car and asked, "Where to?"

I told him my address and we took off, neither of us saying a word the whole way. I was too busy thinking how things were really *really* over between us to say anything and I knew he had to be tired from his tournament. When he pulled into a parking space at the apartment complex I started to take off his hoodie.

"Keep it," he muttered.

No way could I keep it. All it'd do was remind me he'd never be mine. "I can't."

I felt his intense gaze on me. "You can."

I sighed and sat back in my seat and turned my head so I could look at him. "You confuse the hell out of me, Ryker."

One side of his delectable mouth twitched. "Why?"

I turned away and looked down at my hands that were messing with the zipper on the hoodie as I talked. "All I've been for you is a hookup," I glanced at him then looked back at my lap. "But I feel like you're saying one thing and your actions are saying something else."

He ran his hands over his face again with a sigh then put a hand on the back of my seat as he turned toward me. "Would it help if I told you that you confuse the ever-loving fuck out of me too?"

I jerked my head back with a frown as I looked at him. "I do?" I mean, I thought I'd made it perfectly clear what I wanted, having jumped into bed with him twice already. Ergh.

He bit his lip as he nodded slowly. Next, he reached out with the hand on my seat and grabbed a lock of my hair between his fingers and tugged. "You're a huge distraction."

"I am?" This was definitely shocking news.

His eyes moved to the tress he was twisting in his fingers and he snorted. "Oh, yeah."

Okay. Time to end this. We were never going to be together and I needed to move on before he hurt me even worse.

Before I could open my door, he suddenly dug his entire hand into the hair at the back of my head clenching his fingers tightly into it which didn't hurt as much as it startled me, making me cry out. Jerking me toward him roughly, his eyes looked angry. My hands flew out seeking to balance myself before they landed on his muscular thigh, the denim of his jeans now like a second skin on the hard contours of his bent leg and then his face was in mine, his other hand coming up to hold my chin with fingers that gripped firmly as he growled irritably, "Huge fuckin' distraction."

Um. Okay.

"You're confusing me again," I whispered.

His eyes burned hotly into mine at that but I wasn't scared. Matter of fact, I was so turned on I was panting waiting to see what he'd do next.

"In my head all fuckin' day and night, totally fuckin' shit up," he mumbled.

Well, that didn't sound good.

I tried pulling back but he kept me where I was, his fingers digging into my hair and chin a little harder. As he stared me down, I saw him shake his head as if in defeat before smashing his lips against mine in a bruising kiss, his tongue plundering my mouth, finding mine to tangle with it.

Good lord, the man could kiss. I felt a huge dip in my womb at the hunger he displayed as if he couldn't get enough of me. But I was the same (damn it), moving a hand up to lock in his hair, my other behind his neck holding him tightly to me needing more. Always needing more.

We made out for a long time before he ended it (damn it again) with several soft, sweet kisses on my lips, my jaw, my forehead, the tip of my nose.

I was *this* close to asking him in when he spoke up.

"I need your number." He moved his hand from my chin slowly down over my throat, and even more slowly down between my breasts on to my waist and around to my back where he found my pocket and pulled my phone out. He brushed his lips over mine as he handed it to me before sitting back. "Dial," he ordered and gave me a number.

I frowned at his bossiness but dialed the number and upon hearing his phone ring, I hung up.

"Call me anytime you need me," he announced which I thought was really nice. Until he added, "You get starved for my cock, hit me up, babe."

Wow.

Wow.

And here I thought we'd made some leeway but apparently not. I was back to my original play of getting out of his car which I did quickly, but not before turning and telling him to go fuck himself then slamming his door and stomping to mine. Right before I got the key in my door, I heard him chuckle as he said out of his window, "Won't be fuckin' myself, but I will be fuckin' you soon, darlin'."

"Don't hold your breath," I mumbled turning the key in my door. I slammed it too then holding both hands up, fists clenched, I let out a pissed off shriek as I heard him drive off. "Why am I so stupid?" I yelled to no one before stomping to my room and throwing myself on my bed.

My phone chimed that I had a text and I remembered that I needed to text Sharee and Gladys. I was on my stomach, so lifting my head, I swiped my phone unlocked and read what'd been sent.

Text Message—Sun, Jan 18, 12:24 a.m.

Unknown: Don't forget to put my name in your phone, Francesca

Ha. Fat chance of that ever happening. I deleted the text and the number, texted Sharee to let her know I was home then got my pjs and went to take a shower. Back in my room, I heard my phone chime again and picking it up saw I had messages.

Text Message—Sun, Jan 18, 12:57 a.m.

Ree: K! Glad & I are having fun… don't wait up

At least someone was having fun at the party. I looked at the next text.

Text Message—Sun, Jan 18, 12:32 a.m.

Unknown: Goodnight, beautiful

Deleted.

I got in bed and turned out the light only to toss and turn for a while. As I thought about everything, I figured it was good that Ryker pissed me off so much which took the focus off my broken heart.

Would you look at me being all optimistic and shit.

~*~*~*~

I drove Gladys to the airport Sunday morning. She and Sharee had barely gotten up before we had to leave, both of them having hangovers from hell.

"I told you not to let me drink more wine," Gladys whined at Sharee who was practically passed out in the backseat.

Sharee moaned, "As if I could've stopped you," but it came out garbled.

I picked up coffees at Starbucks on the way trying to sober up their drunk asses and by the time we reached the airport, what do you know? They were at least able to walk without zigzagging too much.

"Let me know when the next big party is," Gladys said, hugging both Sharee and me. When she pulled back, she gave me serious eyes. "And I'm sorry I was such a pain in the ass about guys. You're doing just fine, Frankie."

Ugh. If she only knew. But it was still nice to hear she was dropping my love life as her focus for now.

"Yeah," Sharee added. "Sorry, Frank."

"Can I get my phone out and record both of you saying this?" I asked with a grin.

"Hell no," Gladys said with a snicker. "I'm still drunk. I don't know what the fuck I'm saying."

Sharee nodded in agreement and I rolled my eyes at both of them.

"'Kay! I'm outta here! You guys be good!" Gladys announced giving us both a hasty hug before going through security. She turned and gave us one last wave and then she was gone.

"Makes me sad when she's gone," Sharee declared as we turned to leave.

"Yeah," I concurred. "I miss her."

Back at the apartment, Sharee went back to bed while I did laundry and prepared for the coming week. I had minimal lesson plans to write up for PE and only needed to wash jeans to wear, so I was finished in no time. I checked the grocery list on the fridge and decided to do some shopping. Knowing Mrs. Bertolini probably needed a few things, I climbed the stairs to her apartment and knocked on the door.

"Hello, Francesca!" she exclaimed when she opened her door. "Come on in!"

I loved Mrs. B's apartment. It always had a faint smell of Chanel No° 5 with a hint of bread baking, her artwork displayed on every wall and sculptures in every corner. I'd spent an entire afternoon and into the evening with her a couple years ago learning about each piece she'd done and it'd been fascinating. She'd sold a lot of them, having posted them on a website her daughter, who lived in San Francisco, had set up for her several years before and they sold well into the thousands. She'd tried giving me a painting before I left that day, but I'd refused telling her I'd have enough money to buy one some day soon.

"Hi, Mrs. Bertolini. I'm going to the grocery store and wanted to know if you needed anything?"

"I do! But come in and have a cup of tea with me first."

Sharee and I tried visiting with her at least once a week since she lived alone, but she was so busy with the senior center and managing her website that she was in no way lonely.

"What're you hooked on this week?" I asked with a smile since she was always changing her flavors.

"An apple cinnamon herbal that's to die for!"

"Sounds great! I'll get it started." I'd been by so often that I knew where she kept everything. I mean, it wasn't hard since the teakettle was always on the stovetop, but I knew the tea was in the cabinet to the left of the oven and the cups and spoons were on the right.

As I filled the kettle with water she jumped right in. "So who was that young man you were kissing last night?" I turned to her, mouth dropped wide open. "It's not polite to let your mouth hang open, dear." She winked and gave a little chuckle.

"How could you see that?" I asked, putting the kettle on the burner and turning it on. "And what were you doing up that late?"

She chuckled louder. "You forget I've got twenty-twenty vision and I was still awake getting some paintings ready to ship."

I shook my head and leaned against the counter, arms across my chest. "He's just a guy I know."

"From the way it looked, he's more than that to you."

I shrugged. "I'd like for him to be but he doesn't want more." I got the teacups and saucers out of the cabinet and put them on the counter. "Besides, he says the crudest things anyway."

As I got spoons out of the drawer, she answered, "And he looked like he wanted more too, honey. Men don't grab onto a woman the way he was holding you without it meaning something."

Hm.

"And he's a dirty talker too... my Marco had a filthy mouth which added so much to our sex life. Spicy!"

Oh, my God. I actually dropped the box of tea on the floor and couldn't help wanting to put my fingers in my ears and chant a ditty so I didn't hear any more of what she had to say.

She laughed. "I know I'm 'grossing you out' but I'm telling you, when Marco and I were younger, we sure had some good times in bed. You find yourself a dirty talker and you'll never be bored. My first husband was—"

I gasped. "You were married before?" I picked up the box and set it on the counter, opening it to get the bags out to place in our cups.

She nodded. "Yes. To a very nice young man. We were eighteen, in love and couldn't wait any longer. We were both each other's first and it was… nice but not steamy."

The teakettle started whistling so I took it off the burner and poured the hot water into our cups. After putting it back, I carried both cups to the table as Mrs. B followed.

"Now, I was in it for life," she said as she sat. "I'd said those vows in front of God and everyone and I meant them." She picked up her cup and saucer and after blowing on the tea, took a sip. "Joe didn't take them as seriously as I did and ended up having several affairs."

"What?" It pissed me off that someone would treat sweet Mrs. B that way no matter how long ago it was.

She nodded and took another sip. "Oh, we were quite the scandalous couple in town. One just didn't get divorced back then, but I'm not one to put up with a cheating husband, so I went to my father and informed him what was going on. My father was a good man. Honest. Hardworking. He owned a lumber mill in town and people liked him. Respected him. Needless to say, they were quite shocked when he hunted Joe down after giving him a week to stop what he was doing, mind you, and beat the hell out of him."

"Good," I declared before taking a sip.

She chuckled. "And this is where it gets good," she said cryptically giving me a wink before taking a drink.

"What happened?"

"My father wasn't a very big man, standing maybe five-foot-three. Momma barely cleared five feet which is why I'm short. Anyway, Joe was over six feet tall and was a fairly muscular man. People talked at first, but then assumed that Daddy had been just angry enough to best Joe. Oh! I forgot I have Nook pastries! They'd go well with the tea."

I got up and found the pastries in the cabinet, getting a knife out to split one between us. "Go on. I wanna know what happened!"

She smiled then continued as I placed each half on the saucers I'd gotten out. "I'd been around the mill all my life. Daddy was always hiring what Momma called vagabonds, drifters. I'd seen the latest drifter he'd hired months before I learned of Joe's infidelities, and if I hadn't been married, I'd have been all over that."

I laughed at her lingo. I know she'd heard Sharee and me saying that very thing. I took a bite of my pastry half, closing my eyes for a moment at the deliciousness, then opened them to see her doing the same which made me chuckle before I prodded, "And?"

She took another drink. "This drifter was as big as Joe, maybe a tad taller, but he was a Greek god compared. Oh, my, was he handsome. And Daddy liked him because he worked hard too. I'd moved back in with my parents and Momma invited this gorgeous man, Marco, to dinner several times a week since he was renting a room in the hotel and lived alone. I had the biggest crush on him but since I was newly divorced, it was inappropriate to even think of dating anyone at the time, so I waited. After seeing Marco up close, Joe became just a fleeting memory for me. A few months later, we learned Joe had gotten himself in trouble when he had an affair with a married woman whose husband didn't take too kindly to that sort of behavior. That beating landed Joe in the hospital. I went to visit him only out of propriety but wished I hadn't. He had a broken arm, his nose was smashed and it seemed he had bruises everywhere. When I walked into the room, he started crying, asking my forgiveness, begging me to take him back."

"You didn't, though, right?"

Another cryptic smile and more pastry eating and tea sipping was about to drive me to the brink.

"Mrs. B! What happened?" I pleaded for her to continue.

After dabbing her lips with her napkin, she said, "I told the son of a bitch to get lost."

I burst out laughing because she rarely used foul language. I think I'd heard her say damnation once but that was about as bad as it got. Through my giggles I asked, "And you and Marco got together after that?"

"Oh, no, honey. It wasn't that easy."

"Why?"

"I was a divorcée after all and, well, you just didn't hop into another relationship back then."

"So what happened next?"

"Daddy had given me a job keeping the books at the mill so I saw Marco every day and we became friends. We flirted like crazy but nothing ever came of it. Until six months into my working there when he cornered me in the back one day."

Sounding like a broken record, I repeated, "What happened?"

"It was the summer of 1953 and there wasn't air conditioning at the mill. I'd gone to the back to cool off since there was a big fan back there. I'd also grabbed a cup of ice. Since it was hot, I had on a pair of shorts and a button up shirt but I untucked my shirt and had unbuttoned the top several buttons and was smoothing ice over stomach and what would be called my décolletage when Marco happened to walk in and see me. We stared at each other for a moment before he stalked over backing me against the wall and in his slight Italian accent murmured in my ear that he could make me wet in other places."

I gasped again. "Whoa. That was pretty risqué for back then, right?"

"Downright salacious," she said with a smirk.

"So you went out with him after that, right?" She shook her head. "What? Are you kidding me?"

"Nope. We went another six months, casting surreptitious glances at each other, me blushing every time because I knew exactly what he wanted. When finally one night at dinner Marco was over, he looked at my father and said, 'Mr. Williams, I'd like your blessing to date Sarah. Now, we can do this the easy way with you approving or we can go the difficult route with you telling me no and I'll take her out anyway. It's up to you, sir, which way things will go.'"

"Holy shit."

She nodded. "Daddy squinted his eyes at Marco for several seconds, sizing him up, I suppose, then he looked at me. 'What do you say, Sarah?' he asked. I nodded slowly, still in awe that Marco had stood up to Daddy like that."

"Why did you need your dad's permission? You'd already been married before. You were a grown woman, right?"

"I was twenty at the time but still living under my parents' roof." At my questioning look she explained, "That's just how things were back then."

"Weird."

She chuckled. "I guess it would seem weird to today's twenty year olds."

I nodded in agreement. "Okay, go on."

"Marco and I dated for two months before he told me it was he who'd beaten up Joe and not my father. He said the first time he'd seen me he'd been smitten but had been disappointed to learn that I was married. When he found out that Joe was stepping out on me, it infuriated him that he'd do that to me. He approached Daddy and asked if he could take care of it and Daddy was more than happy to allow it." She took a sip of tea. "I'm sure it sounds uncivilized, but in those days people took care of their problems and moved on. We didn't worry about being sued over every little thing. The minute Marco told me he'd been the one to fight for my honor, well, I didn't think it possible to fall more in love with him, but he proved me wrong. Two months later, he proposed, after having gotten Daddy's permission to do so, of course. We got married that spring, a simple ceremony since it was my second marriage, but my dress was still stunning. I remember being so nervous on our wedding night."

I jerked my head back in surprise. "You hadn't slept with him?"

"No. Those were different times, remember? Oh, but we did plenty of other things." At my raised eyebrows she actually giggled. Then she got a faraway look in her eyes. "We were together for fifty-four years before he passed."

I sat watching her get teary-eyed and had to join her. I pulled a paper napkin out of the holder at the center of the table and wiped under my eyes. "That's a beautiful story."

She wiped at her own tears nodding in agreement and went back to her original point. "And let me tell you, the man knew how to talk in bed. So, honey, if you find that, you'd better grab on for dear life."

Now I was crying for real.

"What is it, sweetheart?" She reached over and put her hand on mine, squeezing. I stared down at it while tears ran down my face. Her hand was worn and wrinkled, a few liver spots here and there, fingers crumpled permanently due to the arthritis with which she'd been afflicted. Yet at one point I knew those hands had been capable of creating the most amazing art, they were experienced, had once held babies, wiped runny little noses, blood from scraped knees. They'd comforted a husband when his parents had passed, framed his face when he doubted himself, held his hand as he'd taken his last breath.

I looked up at her. "I love your hands. They're beautiful."

She gave mine another squeeze then smiled waiting for me to talk.

I gave her hand a squeeze back before sliding it out from under hers so I could wipe my eyes again. "I—I don't know if I'll ever have that with someone, that connection," was my choked confession.

She looked affronted. "Honey, you already have a connection like that."

"Yes, but he doesn't want it."

"He looked like he wanted it last night."

I let out a humorless laugh. "He wanted something all right just not that." I looked at her through what I knew were puffy eyes. "He's not interested in a long-term thing. He just wants a hookup."

She nodded knowingly. "A booty call."

I snorted out a real laugh this time. "Mrs. B, how do you know what a booty call is?"

"I may be old but I'm not dead, Francesca." She gave me a discerning look.

"Sorry. Well, it's over between us anyway so it doesn't do any good to talk about it." The look on her face remained. "What?"

"Remember what I told you the other night?"

I nodded. "You said I needed to play it smart if I wanted his eyes to open."

"That's right."

I sighed. "But what does that mean?"

She shrugged. "That's for you to find out."

I stood grabbing up both of our cups and saucers to take to the sink. I rinsed the dishes and put them in the dishwasher then looked back at her. "I just don't think we're meant to be."

She tsk'd at me. "You remember what I said I did to catch Marco's eye?"

I thought for a second, leaning a hip against the counter. "You didn't really do anything."

"Exactly."

"So I'm not supposed to do anything and he'll come around?"

"I didn't say that." She sighed. "You kids today just don't get the nuances anymore. Everything has to be spelled out for you." She winked so I knew she was teasing. "I kept Marco engaged, intrigued. We became friends first but we also flirted a lot and it worked out."

"I'm supposed to become his friend?" I raised an eyebrow.

"What's wrong with that? If you're not friends and you get married, what do you have to fall back on?"

"So am I supposed to text him and stuff?"

"Sure. You're a smart girl. You'll figure it out."

"But what if I become his friend and he starts talking to me about other women?" Yikes. That would suck big time.

"Then you'll know." Her eyes twinkled at me when she said, "But I doubt he's that stupid."

With a sigh I declared, "I'll give it a go and see where it goes."

"Good for you!" she gave me a smile as she stood. "The grocery list is on the fridge. You're a good girl, Francesca. Now, all this talk has worn me out. I'm going to lie down. You've got a key, so let yourself in when you get back."

She turned to go to her room but I called her name, going up to her and bending low gave her a hug. "Thank you."

When I pulled back, she gave my forearms a squeeze. "Any time, dear."

Monday morning I was ready to start a new flirty friendship with Ryker but Coach G informed me he'd be gone all week for a wrestling matches. Damn. The kids were out of school for MLK, Jr. Day, so we had a professional development day and I'd looked forward to getting to sit by him and flirt a little. Maybe next time.

Tuesday I'd resolved to text him. The Friday before, I'd started bringing a sack lunch and eating in Coach G's office since I only got twenty-five minutes and the cafeteria was on the other side of campus. I'd gone there the first two days but by the time I stood in line then got my tray, I had five minutes to eat and get back. Coach G went home for lunch, so I had the office to myself and decided I'd text Ryker to get the friendship/flirting ball rolling. I'm not going to mention that my hands were shaking so badly that I almost dropped my phone in my cup of ramen instant lunch thingy.

I scrolled through my contacts and found MFRyker which stood for "My Friend Ryker" to remind me what Mrs. B had told me. I also kind of got a kick out of the fact that it looked like something else especially since he'd been a jerk the last time I saw him.

Text Message—Tues, Jan 20, 11:14 a.m.

Me: Hi. It's Frankie. I just wanted to wish you luck at your match. Also, you'd have been proud of Jack, the little third grader with brown hair who's already got more muscles than I do, because he asked Coach G if they could wrestle like Coach Powers does. Okay, well, take care

Holy shit that was nerve-racking. I was sure he was busy and wouldn't text back until later so I was surprised when my phone chimed right away.

Text Message—Tues, Jan 20, 11:14 a.m.

MFRyker: Hey Francesca. Thanks for the luck but it takes skill and strength to win, which I'll be doing at the end of each match. Tell Jack he's badass. You wearing that sweet little t-shirt today that makes your tits look so fucking good?

Wow. Did I really want to be friends with this guy much less try to get in a relationship with him? I knew he was just being an ass on purpose. His teammates were probably around so he was trying to be cool. Jerk.

I tried maintaining a light and flirty disposition but I could feel it slipping because he riled me up more than any other person I'd known.

Text Message—Tues, Jan 20, 11:16 a.m.

Me: You're definitely confident in yourself. I hope that works for you. I'll be sure to tell Jack you approve.

A couple seconds later he texted back.

Text Message—Tues, Jan 20, 11:16 a.m.

MFRyker: Shirt? Tits? Good? C'mon, sweetheart. I wanna know

Flirty, flirty, flirty. Must maintain flirty attitude.

Fuck that. I could sense the tone behind his *sweetheart* and it wasn't nice.

Text Message—Tues, Jan 20, 11:16 a.m.

Me: I've got on the shirt. Do you have on the sweet little singlet that displays your package so nicely, SWEETHEART?

Let's see how he liked being objectified.

Text Message—Tues, Jan 20, 11:16 a.m.

MFRyker: Have you been checking out my package? If so, you'd know my singlet is not little because of the size of my package alone, SWEETHEART

Dear God. I'd thought Mrs. B had something here, I mean, it'd been better advice than what Sharee and Gladys had given me, but still. I began to think I'd bitten off more than I could chew. Ugh.

Text Message—Tues, Jan 20, 11:17 a.m.

Me: Well, I need to go. The kids will be coming in soon

Text Message—Tues, Jan 20, 11:17 a.m.

MFRyker: Your lunch is over at 11:30. You've still got time. I want an answer

Text Message—Tues, Jan 20, 11:17 a.m.

Me: An answer to what?

Playing dumb was my only out.

Text Message—Tues, Jan 20, 11:17 a.m.

MFRyker: You know, I'm not gonna make you answer because I know you've checked it out up close and personal. Fuck. I can't wait to get up close and personal with you again

God. I'd be willing to bet Mrs. B and her husband's flirting never got this graphic. I sat staring at his message not knowing what to say. Did I say I couldn't wait either only to find out I was still just a hookup? Did I tell him he'd have to work for it first?

Man, I sucked at this so bad.

Instead of answering, I let time run out before texting him back, coward that I was.

Text Message—Tues, Jan 20, 11:27 a.m.

*Me: I've really got to go. Good luck! Let me know how you do!
<3*

Text Message—Tues, Jan 20, 11:27 a.m.

MFRyker: Coward... Gonna call tonight at 11. Be ready

Be ready? What'd that mean? I was definitely afraid to find out.

~*~*~*~

I hate when people give you a time for something because when the time passes, you get all nervous and jumpy wondering if they forgot or they were just joking or they were setting you up to make you look like an idiot, and then each minute past the time takes an hour to go by.

All these things were running through my mind that night as I lay in bed when I looked at my phone for the thousandth time.

11:08 p.m.

Now to figure out which of the aforementioned Ryker was pulling. All three worked but I hoped it was option four: He'd been so tired from competing he'd fallen asleep.

At 11:11 p.m. I decided I didn't care anymore. There was no doubt in my mind that he'd played me and I was the fool who'd fallen for it.

11:16 p.m. and I was pissed for even checking my phone again.

By 11:21 p.m. I was done. My feelings were hurt and I knew if I checked my fucking phone again I'd probably start crying. I turned off the ringer and put it on my nightstand and just as I turned to go to sleep, my phone started buzzing.

Shit.

I can't explain what went on in my head (and stupid heart) when I saw *MFRyker Calling* on the screen. Excitement. Anger. Elation. Relief.

I slid my finger across the screen and answered, "Hello?"

"Hey. Sorry I'm late. Fuckin' Martinez took for fuckin' ever to get out of the locker room then we stopped and ate then Coach had a meeting in his hotel room. I just got out."

"Oh," I whispered.

"Where are you?"

"In bed," I answered which made me shiver for some reason.

"Mmm... good."

I could hear talking in the background. "Where are you?"

"In my hotel room. Rooks, my roommate, is staying in his girlfriend's room." Ah. The talking was the TV.

"Isn't that against the rules?" I asked.

He chuckled. "Yeah. Only if he gets caught, though."

"Oh. So how'd you do today?"

"Pinned my opponent in the second period. He was pissed too. All-American last two years, thought he was the shit. You should've seen the look on his face when the ref blew the whistle. Priceless."

I laughed. "I'll bet. Good for you, Ryker. Congratulations."

"Thanks, Francesca."

"Um, I don't really understand wrestling since I was always playing basketball, so don't think I'm dumb if I ask the wrong questions."

"I'd never think you're dumb. Ask whatever you want and I'll answer."

"Okay. So do you wrestle again tomorrow?"

"No, not until Thursday then again on Saturday. This is some tri-state thing that we do every year. Washington, Oregon, Idaho. This year we're in Portland. Last year it was at home. Year before it was in Boise. We stay the week and all three schools compete against each other."

"That sounds like a good idea but I'll bet you're tired when you get back," I said.

"It's tiring just like a tournament but not too bad. We've got managers who do all our laundry and we get fed, so we've got it pretty good."

"What hotel are you staying at?"

"The Radisson which is pretty nice."

"Oh, good." I thought I heard him lying on the bed. "So I didn't get to tell you the other night that I met your brother, Loch. If he hadn't told me you were older, I'd have thought you were twins."

He chuckled. "People are always saying that. Before Zeke and Gable graduated, they were always mixing us up."

"You have three brothers? And you all look alike?"

"Yep."

"So the Powers brothers have had all the women at Hallervan mesmerized for going on six years now?"

He barked out a laugh. "Mesmerized, huh? Do I have you mesmerized, Francesca?"

My toes curled at hearing him laugh and at how deep his voice was. Gah. "I'd have to say you do, Ryker. And most people call me Frankie."

"I like Francesca. So tell me how I have you mesmerized."

I bit my lip unsure what I should tell him. I tried channeling a young Mrs. B to see what she'd say. She sounded like she'd been pretty feisty when she was younger, was probably pretty straightforward, so I tried going with that.

"I've always wanted to know you, but you seemed untouchable so I stayed away." I didn't tell him about our getting married and having three kids since it'd probably scare him off which made me snort.

"You stayed away?"

"Well, yeah, until your party." My face flushed just thinking of that night.

"Mmm… the party. That was a good night."

I laughed. "You practically kicked me out of your bed. And then you didn't even remember me."

"I remembered you."

I rolled my eyes. "You were making out with that stripper chick with the VW Bug when I came by."

I heard him let out a breath. "Why *did* you come by?"

"My roommate talked me into asking you out." He was quiet for so long I thought he may have fallen asleep. "Ryker?"

"Fucked that up, didn't I?"

I shrugged as I lay there. "Yeah, but everything happens for a reason."

I heard him shift in the bed. "I meant what I said that morning."

I closed my eyes, remembering as another shiver ran through me.

"Baby, I meant it when I said you were the best."

My breathing sped up and I barely got out, "Yeah?"

"Yeah. Tell me what you're wearing," he rumbled, his voice suddenly all husky and sexy.

Well, he wasn't wasting any time here, was he? But, by God, I suddenly found I was all in, finished with trying to be feisty and probably not accomplishing it anyway.

"A tank top and shorts."

"Can you do something for me?" he asked.

"What?" I breathed.

"Can you put your hand under your tank top…"

"Yes," I whispered, throwing my covers back and doing as he said.

"Now move it up to your gorgeous tit and run your thumb over your nipple."

"Okay," I breathed out.

"Use your thumb and finger now. Roll it between them. Imagine it's my mouth on it, sucking hard, licking, kissing, flicking my tongue over it."

A moan escaped as I pictured him doing all of that. God.

"That's it, baby. Do the same to your other breast now." I knew he could hear me panting when he said, "Good girl." That was a huge turn-on making me arch up off the bed letting out a soft moan. "Now move your hand down over your belly… down inside your shorts, inside your panties and touch yourself."

"Ryker," I moaned turning my head to the side and my face was in his hoodie I'd hung on my bedpost. God. I reached for it with the hand that held my phone, pulling it down so I could smell it, him. That amped things up fast and another low moan slid from my throat.

"Fuck," I heard him mutter. "You rubbing your clit, Francesca?"

"Yes."

"Put a finger inside yourself. Tell me how wet you are for me."

"So wet, God, so wet for you..."

"Mmm... put another finger inside and move them in and out." At my gasp, he ordered, "Now put another finger in. Imagine it's my cock stroking inside you."

I heard him groan and realized he had to be touching himself too. The image that came to mind made my body tremble as I felt my orgasm building. "Oh, my God," I moaned loudly.

"Fuck yourself with your fingers, baby. That's me fucking you right now, fucking you so hard," he growled.

And just imagining that got me there. "I'm gonna come!" I cried, pumping my fingers harder, picturing him above me, his hips driving into mine, his big shaft thrusting in so deep. A wave of euphoria immediately shot through me as I climaxed, my hips bowing up off the bed as my fingers went deep.

I heard him bite out another "Fuck!" and knew he was coming too which was so erotic I felt another wave blast through me causing my toes to curl, my body to lock up for a moment before I collapsed on the bed breathing hard. Holy damn.

I listened to him breathing just as hard as I was then heard him say, "You there?"

"Yes," I answered between breaths.

"God, you turn me the fuck on, Francesca," he rasped.

Even though I was thoroughly physically wasted at the moment, I mentally did a freaking happy dance.

"You kinda do that to me too, Ryker," I responded breathily.

"Hang on," he said. I heard him get up then water was running and I knew he was cleaning himself off which made me smile that I'd made him come too. I grabbed the hoodie and pulled it to my face, breathing in deep. Damn. "Back," he remarked a minute later and I heard him getting back in bed.

"Hi," I whispered.

"Hey," he answered right back. "So tell me about your family. Any brothers or sisters?"

"Nope. I'm an only child."

He laughed. "I wouldn't even have known how to feel if I didn't have my brothers."

"It was lonely sometimes but I always had friends over, so it wasn't too bad."

"Have you always live in Seattle?" he inquired.

I told him about living in Texas before moving before my sophomore year in high school. I learned he'd been born and raised here and he now knew I'd been an All-American basketball player before tearing up my knee.

We talked until four in the morning and the only reason he let me go was that I'd accidentally fallen asleep but had awoken suddenly, apologizing to him.

"You get your rest, baby," he whispered. "You've got to deal with kids tomorrow."

"Okay. 'Night," I whispered back.

"'Night, beautiful," he replied and then he was gone.

I curled into my covers and fell asleep with a huge smile on my face.

11—Danger Position

My classes were great the rest of the week and the kids had learned to call me Coach M which was a lot easier for them. My night class was going well also. Monday night we hadn't had class because of the holiday, but Wednesday night I not only learned how to tape jammed fingers but I mastered taping shin splints too. Before class ended Wednesday, Coach Nolan told us that the next several Wednesdays he was going to have athletes come in to talk about their previous injuries. As I was walking out, he called me over and asked if I'd speak about my torn ACL which was cool.

Ryker and I texted the rest of the week off and on and I was thrilled that Mrs. B's advice was working, even though I'm sure she would've frowned at the phone sex, but that'd been an error on my part. I'd be focusing on the flirty friend part from now on hoping the phone sex had been the intrigue.

He texted Thursday that he'd won his second match by a technical fall, whatever that was. He'd tried explaining through texts, something about fifteen points from near falls which he also tried explaining, telling me his opponent's head was on the mat and he'd gotten the guy's shoulder at a forty-five degree angle to it and held it for five seconds so he'd gotten three points and I was so confused. But I'd texted him lots of celebration emojis in return and he'd texted back calling me a dork.

Friday night he told me he wouldn't be able to text much on Saturday because after his match his coach had asked him to help out which Ryker was totally pumped about. He said he'd be home Sunday night and would text once he got in.

Saturday, I was pretty bored. I really wished I'd stayed at Nordstrom and asked to work on weekends. To fill the time, Sharee and I did a little shopping Saturday then came home for a marathon of *The Office* on Netflix and argued for an hour over whether John Krasinski was cute or not. I said yes, she said no, I finally pointed out that if Emily Blunt married him there was something there and she finally conceded.

Sunday Sharee went to my parents' with me for dinner. I'd made her promise not to say anything about my love life and she'd held strong until Mom sneakily asked what our Valentines were getting us and Sharee had blurted that she wouldn't be getting anything but I possibly could. I berated her asking how in the world was she going to be a lawyer if she couldn't even fend off a cross-examination from my mom. We were home by eight which gave me plenty of time to make up lesson plans for the week, throw in a load of laundry and make brownies. After taking a shower and getting into bed, my phone chimed.

> *Text Message—Sun, Jan 25, 11:14 p.m.*
>
> *MFRyker: You still up?*
>
> *Text Message—Sun, Jan 25, 11:14 p.m.*
>
> *Me: Yep. Just lying in bed counting sheep*
>
> *Text Message—Sun, Jan 25, 11:14 p.m.*
>
> *MFRyker: If I were there, you'd be counting orgasms*

Oh my.

> *Text Message—Sun, Jan 25, 11:15 p.m.*
>
> *Me: I'd probably lose count like before...*
>
> *Text Message—Sun, Jan 25, 11:15 p.m.*
>
> *MFRyker: Fuck yeah you would*

Feisty but friends only, Frankie!

> *Text Message—Sun, Jan 25, 11:15 p.m.*
>
> *Me: So you'll be at school tomorrow?*

Text Message—Sun, Jan 25, 11:16 p.m.

MFRyker: Until lunch then I have practice

Text Message—Sun, Jan 25, 11:16 p.m.

Me: Who'd you have to blow to work out THAT schedule?

There. That was feisty. I giggled to myself waiting for him to answer.

Waiting.

Waiting some more.

And still waiting.

Great. I'd pissed him off with my feistiness.

I sat up in bed biting my lip wondering what to do. I wished I could run up and ask Mrs. B but she was probably in bed already and if not, she'd most certainly gripe me out for being so crude. When he still didn't answer more than ten minutes later, I shrugged. Whatever. If he was that sensitive and that big of a baby then screw him, right?

I lay back down and just as I set my phone on my nightstand it rang. Ryker. Eep!

"Hello?" I answered.

"Who'd I have to blow?"

I couldn't help the snort I let out at hearing him say that but I quickly covered it up. "It was a joke… you know, as in ha ha, funny?"

"*Sweetheart*, I don't know if you remember correctly, but the only one who's getting blown around here is me."

Ugh. There was the *sweetheart* again and what'd he mean by that? Was he meaning me or all the other women he'd slept with? Ugh.

Italian temper kicking in in three... two...

"Oh, I'm sure, *sweetheart*. You probably had women lined up all week wanting to blow you, didn't you?"

Shit. This is not where I was wanting this to go.

He let out a laugh and fired back, "Every fuckin' night. They couldn't get enough of my cock."

"Fuck you, Ryker."

"Fuck me? About to make that happen, *sweetheart*."

Wait, what? It was then I realized there were car noises in the background so he was driving. Duh. And now my stomach dropped because he'd just admitted he was on his way to sleep with another woman.

God.

God!

"Yeah, well, I hope you have fun," I bit out hearing his car door open then close. "Do me a favor and lose my number."

I hung up disgusted at how things had just gone, hurt that he'd flaunted that shit right in my face and angry at myself for even trying to be his friend in the first place. Tossing my phone onto my nightstand I lay back in bed staring at the ceiling and felt a tear run down the side of my face. I wiped it away angrily then lay there wondering if I could be relocated for student teaching. But that pissed me off more since I'd been there first. If anyone should have to leave, it should be Ryker. I was thinking of how I could make that happen when there was a knock at the front door the same time a text came through.

Text Message—Sun, Jan 25, 11:41 p.m.

MFRyker: Answer your door, SWEETHEART

~*~*~*~

I jumped out of bed and ran to the front door before Sharee woke up. Unlocking it then yanking it open, I looked up at Ryker who had his arms stretched up, his hands resting at the top of the doorframe, knee bent, but he wasn't looking at me. He was staring at the ground, the hood of his jacket pulled up and hiding his face. His hoodie was unzipped and I saw that he wore a wife beater underneath, stretched tight over his muscular chest.

I heard him blow out a breath then his head came up and he looked at me, his golden eyes boring into mine with intense broodiness. Jeez. When his tongue moved to touch his back molar, his mouth going askew, I knew he was pissed. Well, so was I.

"Lose your number?" he finally asked, his eyes glittery as they held mine.

I leaned forward and snapped, "They couldn't get enough of your cock?"

He moved fast, arms coming down from the doorframe and stepping inside, he bent to put his shoulder in my gut and picked me up. He next kicked the door closed behind him twisting to engage the lock before turning back to the living room and asking, "Where's your bedroom."

"What? Put me down!" I hissed as quietly as I could not wanting to wake Sharee, my fists banging against his lower back trying to make him let me go.

Smack!

Oh my God. He'd just spanked me.

"Are you kidding me right now?" I whisper-hissed.

"Where's your fucking bedroom?"

"Put me down!" I demanded, kicking my legs.

Smack!

"Bedroom?"

Holy shit. I knew his stubborn ass wasn't going to put me down, so I snarled, "To the left."

He took off walking, and once inside my room threw me on the bed before turning to shut and lock my door.

"Are you crazy?" I bit off, scrambling to get off my bed on the other side.

"You have no fuckin' idea, *sweetheart*," he said through gritted teeth then grabbed me by the ankle and pulled me back to him.

I twisted around to where I was on my back thinking I could kick him if I needed to, which was a huge mistake because he was fast and it only served to give him a chance to grab my other ankle and pull me harder to him. His hands slid down behind my knees and he jerked my hips up off the bed, spreading my legs and pulling me where they went to either side of his waist.

"What are you doing?" I shrieked when he fell on top of me, pinning me to the bed and pulling my tank top off.

His hand went between us to unbutton his jeans then they were at my shorts, tearing them and my panties down my legs and off while I tried beating him off me with my fists. He had a condom out in no time which he put between his teeth and ripped open, his hood still on his head which gave him a menacing aura. "Tell me you don't want this," he said, his voice gravelly with lust.

I stared up at him and couldn't say the words. They wouldn't come out. Because I did want him. I always wanted him. God.

"Then I'm giving you what you want. What you need," he growled before thrusting inside me so hard it made us both cry out. "Fuck!" he roared as he began driving in, his hips pistoning so powerfully he was heaving me across the bed.

Why did I try fighting him off, how could I have not wanted this? Oh, God. This was good. This was amazing.

I grabbed onto his wrists that were at the sides of my head to hold myself in place as he continued pumping hard. Then wrapping my arms around his broad shoulders and doing the same with my legs around his waist, I began moving my hips up to meet each of his thrusts which coerced a guttural and very sexy groan from him.

"You like that?" I whispered because for once, he was quiet.

"I love... love it," he answered, his voice husky and rough.

Those words... from his mouth... oh God... they made me want to hear him say that about me. To me. I closed my eyes trying to block them out, but the pang they left in my heart made me fail, because I'd already fallen for him and was left only with the hope that he could feel the same.

I arched against him as he filled me again and again, the aching throb between my legs building. And when he slid his hands down under my bottom, wrenching me up hard into him, I was there, his mouth covering mine to swallow my scream as my orgasm tore through me, laying waste to everything in its path until my body went blissfully limp.

"That's my good girl," he groaned.

He pulled out, and leaving me panting on the bed stood to undress quickly before joining me again. Putting my legs around his waist, he thrust deep, so deep, pounding into me over and over until he was there and I watched as every muscle in his neck and chest tightened, the striations popping out to look like bas-relief carved into a sculpture. He threw his head back, his entire body straining as his release overtook him, and slamming inside me several times finally stilled then collapsed on top of me with a grunt.

I'd heard my friends say they hated when a guy laid on them like this because they couldn't breathe, but I loved it with Ryker. Loved taking all his weight because it meant he'd spent every bit of himself on me, given me everything he had. I ran my fingers through his hair that was damp with perspiration, closing my eyes as I breathed him in.

He shifted a bit so I could breathe easier and we lay that way for a long time, our bodies still connected, his arms under me holding me tightly, mine around him, one hand in his hair the other drawing patterns on his back.

He turned his head, first kissing my shoulder a few times then pulling up to lean on his forearm, he looked at me with warm, amber eyes as he smoothed his finger across my bottom lip. "I'll be back," he said, touching his lips to mine before getting up and going in the bathroom.

I watched him go, his tight, muscular ass looking bite-worthy and then there was that scary tattoo across his back looking cruel as always.

When he came back don't think I didn't take the front all in too. I loved his high cheekbones that topped a square jaw making him look like a young Alain Delon in the old Dior Sauvage ad, not the bearded one but the one where Dior Photoshopped out his cigarette. The defined muscles of his chest, arms, abs, the V at his hips, or Adonis Belt they called it, and his strong thighs. Then there were the tattoos, some colorful and some not, each representing passages in his life, I assumed. And finally there was his beautifully perfect, huge, cock that was now semi-erect as he got in bed beside me. Damn.

Leaning down he brushed his lips against mine softly once, twice, three times and then the kiss became something more. It became heated, urgent, feeling so different from his other kisses in that it made me feel as if he owned every bit of me. The possessiveness of it almost symbolic, as if he was marking me somehow, a warning to other men that I was his.

And I loved every single bit of it.

"We do this, we have to have rules, Francesca," he mumbled when he pulled back.

Rules?

I started to ask what he meant but he shushed me, reaching to turn off my bedside lamp then cradling me in his arms as he caressed my neck with soft kisses, whispering sweet nothings in my ear, telling me I was beautiful, that he loved the curve of my back, loved how smart I was, the fact that I could hold my own, the tautness of my tummy before he fell asleep.

And I fell even more in love with him as I listened to his even breaths.

I was so totally screwed.

~*~*~*~

We held hands as I walked him out to his car the next morning at six. I'd pulled on some jeans and his hoodie along and slipped my Keds on. He had on his jeans and hoodie from the night before and in the early morning fog, we must've looked like phantoms.

"Hello, Francesca!" Mrs. Bertolini called from her patio making Ryker stop in his tracks and look behind him then up. Of course with her twenty-twenty vision she'd seen us.

He dropped my hand, turning to face her wrapping his arm around my shoulders and drawing me into him to where my front was against his side. I put an arm across his back and rested the palm of my other against his abs. Tucking his chin to his shoulder he looked down and asked, "Is it okay she saw us or do I need to make her disappear?"

I nodded with a roll of my eyes and smiled up at him, at which he winked then tightening his arm around me he leaned down and kissed the side of my head.

"And who might this be?" Mrs. Bertolini hollered down.

"This is Ryker Powers, Mrs. Bertolini," I said back.

"Hello, Ryker. Oh, my. Aren't you handsome? You remind me of my Marco." I knew she probably couldn't see him too clearly in the lighting but she was not wrong about his being handsome.

Ryker grinned up at her. "It's nice meeting you, Mrs. Bertolini."

"And polite too." She grinned back at him. Then looking at me she added, "I have a good feeling about this young man, Francesca."

Instant face flush since she knew exactly who he was to me. "Uh, okay. I'll talk to you later, Mrs. B."

"Glad to see you kids had some fun!" she chortled before heading back inside her apartment.

Ryker breathed out a chuckle. "I like her." Then he looked down at me and I saw the intensity was back in his eyes. "We need to talk later."

"Okay," I whispered hoping that what was going on between us was what I thought it was.

Taking my hand he pulled me with him to his car. "I'll see you in a bit, okay, baby?"

I nodded and tiptoed up to kiss him, feeling the same possessiveness I'd felt before from him, and loved every bit of it.

"Bye," I said as he got in his car and started it up. He closed his door, gave me a wink, backed out and left.

When I turned to go back to my apartment, I heard a small voice say, "Was that him?"

Mrs. B had come back out on her balcony and I looked up at her answering, "Yes."

"Oh, honey, what you've got is a very good thing. I feel it in my bones."

I smiled goofily up at her, giddy as all get out. "Thank you, Mrs. B. You were so right."

She grinned as she held her coffee cup up as if toasting me. I grinned right back before going inside to get ready for school.

Ryker and I had a blast that day in PE. Coach G had had us lay down mats and he'd gotten out the mini trampolines. The kids loved them. They partnered up and had to do routines to mostly Kidz Bop songs that I played over the speakers, changing songs every few minutes.

In the smaller classes, Coach G told Ryker and me to team up while he manned the music and Ryker had me dying at some of the moves he made. When "Hotline Bling" came on I thought I was going to pee my pants I was laughing so hard. I mean, add Drake's strange dance moves to a mini trampoline and it was hilarious. The coolest part was that Ryker seemed to love making me laugh, not even one bit afraid of making a fool out of himself which was surprising seeing how serious and intense he always was.

The kids loved it too, and it melted my heart watching all the little girls who were totally in love with him (how could they not be?) wanting to dance with him. He never turned them down either, pulling each one up on the trampoline with him and dancing with them. One of the best parts was that he also won over the younger boys when he Whipped and Nae Nae'd and I cried I was laughing so hard.

Right before lunch, the fifth graders were in class and just before the lunch bell, Ryker yelled out, "Sheridan!" He and I were being goofy on our trampoline since it was a small class, and I looked over to see the cute little redheaded girl nod and give him a thumbs up as she ran to her bag. Then she ran to Coach G and handed him a CD telling him which track to play. I looked at Ryker who smirked at me then waggled his eyebrows when "Time of My Life" from the *Dirty Dancing* soundtrack came on.

I shook my head. "Oh, no, we are not reenacting the lift scene," I told him, backing away.

He hooked his finger at me just like Johnny did to Baby when she first went to the workers' dorms in the movie and they were all dancing. Ugh.

"Go, Coach M! Go, Coach M!" the kids were chanting and I smiled, apologetically shaking my head at them.

"Don't tell me you're scared," Ryker taunted. He looked at the kids. "I think Coach M is scared!"

I rolled my eyes but of course the competitor in me hated to lose, so glaring at him, I stated, "You'd better catch me."

"Always," he said with a grin then stepped past the trampoline nodding at it to let me know I was supposed to jump on it then into his arms. Yeesh.

"Fuck," I murmured to myself then blowing out a breath and shaking out my hands, I geared up to do the stupid lift.

The kids were still chanting when I looked at Ryker who nodded for me to go. After wiping my hands on the fronts of my thighs, I took off in a run, hit the trampoline, bounced into the air and right into his strong hands.

"I did it!" I screamed, throwing my arms out what I thought was gracefully which caused him to get off balance and we fell, me landing on top of him in a heap.

The kids were yelling and clapping but promptly ran to the door and out when the bell rang for lunch, leaving us where we were.

"Nice catch," I said, pulling back to look down at Ryker.

"Nice jump. Until it wasn't," he said and we cracked up.

"Getting lunch," Coach G grumbled and left the gym.

Ryker turned us to where he was on top of me and kissed me long and hard then hopped up holding his hand out to help me up.

"I'd say some cheesy parting line, like, I've had the time of my life, or nobody puts Frankie in a corner, but then you'd think I was even more awesome than you already do and I just can't risk it," he said holding my hand as we walked to Coach G's office so he could get his wallet and hoodie.

Inside the office, I snorted. "Riiiight. That might make me fall even more in lo—"

Fuck.

Fuck, fuck, fuck.

I felt my face flush and I became very interested in the calendar that was on Coach's desk.

"Francesca," Ryker called but I wouldn't look at him, having become infatuated with seeing if there was an "I'm an idiot" day. He called my name again after getting his hoodie on and I finally raised my eyes only to see amusement in his. "If I didn't think we'd get caught, I'd fuck you right here on the desk. Maybe against the door. We can do both tonight at my place, though." He wrapped his arms around me and gave me a scorching kiss before he left.

Damn.

~*~*~*~

Pressed against Ryker's bedroom door, my fingers digging into his shoulders while one of his hands held my bottom and the other was between us rubbing circles against me, I cried out his name as my climax hit me.

"God, your pussy is so greedy for me, isn't it, baby? Clamping onto my cock like it's not gonna let go," he mumbled in my ear. Then he moved us away from the door and putting both hands underneath me, lifted me then slammed me down onto his hard cock, doing this over and over. "Fuck me," he groaned, closing his eyes as he kept the movement going. I knew he was close when he slowed his thrusts but deepened them at the same time. "So fuckin' tight. Jesus fuck!" he growled driving me down hard on him as he came.

But then he stumbled and sat down on the edge of his bed saying he was dizzy, wrapping his arms tightly around me and burying his face in my neck, breathing hard.

"You okay?" I asked worriedly after he'd finally caught his breath.

He pulled back and looked at me smoothing my perspiration dampened hair off my forehead. "Yeah. I'm good. Just never came that hard before."

I cupped his face with my hands and kissed him. God. I so totally loved this man.

When the kiss ended, he gently lifted me off him and laid me in the bed, covering me up. "Be back."

When he came back to bed, he gathered me in his arms to face him. "I've got a match here this Thursday night. Will you come?"

A thrill ran through me that he wanted me to watch him. "Of course," I said, gliding my fingers over his cheekbone. "I wouldn't miss it for the world."

He turned his head and kissed my palm. "Good."

~*~*~*~

The next two days in PE were just as fun as Monday. I'd never seen this side of Ryker and I was loving that he was letting loose and having fun. We'd played tag on Tuesday then gotten the parachute out on Wednesday.

Thursday he wasn't there because of the match. His coach wanted him to watch film then they had a team lunch before they had weigh-ins or whatever routine they did before a match.

That night I was nervous because we'd texted Wednesday night after my class and he'd told me his opponent hadn't lost all season. Of course Ryker hadn't sounded like he was worried but I was. I'd been an athlete my entire life and I knew how things worked. The superstitions, the routines, all that stuff that every athlete counted on before each event. When I'd played, I'd had my own little rituals and superstitions, like eating pasta primavera before games so the complex carbs would help sustain my energy and the olive oil worked as an anti-inflammatory. I also never wore an outfit on game day again if I didn't play well when I'd worn it before. Sharee and I had this stupid secret handshake that we did in the locker room before every game which we knew helped us play better. And the entire team had to touch a banner that hung over the locker room door on our way out to the floor or we knew we wouldn't win. Athletes are just weird that way.

That's why I was worried.

What if Ryker didn't do well and he blamed it on my being there to watch. Hey, I'd felt the same when a certain friend would tell me they'd be at my game and if I didn't play well or we lost, I secretly blamed my friend for being there and messing up the mojo.

So, yeah, I was nervous.

Sharee was coming with me but we drove our own cars in case she got bored, as she told me. We got to the gym and found our seats and I was immediately fascinated. Ryker wasn't in the ring yet, in fact, I didn't see him anywhere, but the two guys who were in the ring were grappling hard with each other. I was totally clueless about what was going on but I watched as the guy from Hallervan grabbed the other guy's foot which made him twist and fall to his knees which caused the ref to hold up his hand and two points were put on the board for the Hallervan dude. Hm.

I looked at Sharee out of the corner of my eye and we both shrugged.

While I watched, I learned that wrestling was probably the hardest sport ever because these guys had to be in tremendous shape and not only have physical strength but mental strength as well. At one point, the Hallervan guy was down and the other guy had his leg all twisted around which made Sharee and I both cringe. I mean, ouch.

Halfway through the second period, Sharee nudged me with her elbow and pointed. Following her finger, I saw that Ryker was now on the floor behind the bench wearing a maroon Hallervan warmup suit and he had headgear on so I knew he was probably up next. I couldn't keep my eyes off him as he jogged in place for a while then stretched his legs, first pulling one to his chest then the other. He threw in several more stretches jogging in between time then the horn blew on the clock and I realized the match I'd been watching was over. The ref held up the Hallervan guy's hand, so he'd won but I didn't know why. I'd been too busy watching Ryker.

There was a break while they cleaned the mat and a group of cheerleaders-slash-dancers dressed in short shorts and what looked like sports bras ran in front of the mat and lined up, heads bowed waiting for their music to start. "Call Me Maybe" started playing and the girls' heads popped up and they started doing their moves. It was really cute and I was enjoying it until I noticed a gorgeous blonde girl with a killer body paying particular attention to Ryker. And he was watching her back!

Sharee elbowed me pointing out the now obvious, and we both watched as the girl did the phone thing with her fingers to her ear at the chorus and pointed at Ryker nodding with a smirk. I looked at him to see he was smirking right back.

What?

"Who is that?" I asked.

"I have no idea but I want her waistline."

Yeah, she was totally built and beautiful and I'm sure Ryker had "hit that" at some point. I mean, duh. They'd been watching each other the whole time. Well, during the time that I was watching them watch each other.

When the song was over, the girls did that cheerleader wave thing to the crowd and skipped off the mat screaming, "Go Bulldogs!"

My eyes went back to Ryker and I watched as he came around the bench and pulled off his warmup pants and jacket then bent to check his shoelaces. My God he looked good, all ripped and muscular. Wow. His coach came up and talked to him for a moment before kind of smacking him on the side of the head. Um. Ryker went to the center circle on the mat shaking his legs out then his arms. His opponent joined him and then the ref was there. Ryker and the other guy were in a stance bending at the waist and shook hands just before the ref blew his whistle.

I'm not going to lie. I was about to pull my hair out throughout the entire thing. Right off the bat, Ryker grab the guy and threw him down and I stood up and yelled, "Yeah!" before realizing no one else had stood and I literally had no idea what was going on so I sat back down.

At the end of the first period, Ryker was ahead 1-0 which was good. The second period started and his opponent took the lead immediately, 2-1. I wished I'd known how the scoring worked or what the hell they were doing that was getting them points but I figured I'd learn as things progressed.

I didn't.

By the third period I was confused as ever because although Ryker had picked the guy up a couple times and slammed him down, he'd gotten no points but the guy had when he'd gotten away from him. Weird. Then it happened the opposite way with the opponent kicking

Ryker's feet out from under him and taking him to the floor but Ryker got away from him somehow and was awarded two points.

Throughout there'd been a lot of standstill stuff with Ryker holding this guy down not letting him do anything and I wondered what the point of it was. With fourteen seconds to go, they were tied 4-4 and I'd bitten two of my fingernails to the quick.

"Is it going to end in a tie? Do they have overtime?" I asked Sharee who responded with a shrug. God, we were pathetic.

At five seconds, they'd gone out of the ring and the ref blew his whistle but no score went up. They were still tied. Back in the ring they faced off and the ref blew his whistle then the five seconds went off the clock and the ref whistled again. The Hallervan crowd started cheering but I didn't understand since it was a tie. But then the ref held up Ryker's arm and when I looked at the score, he'd won 5-4. Um, okay. I heard the announcer saying something about riding time, so I guess he'd earned a point somehow.

Anyway, I stood and cheered with everyone else because it was awesome that my guy had won and I watched as he looked up and pointed two fingers at the ceiling but I wasn't sure what that meant.

What wasn't awesome was that I saw the little blonde run out to him and hug him around the neck quickly before disappearing again. What the hell was that?

"Well, that was fun," Sharee announced sarcastically.

"Hey, you got to see hot guys in singlets. You should be happy."

"Meh. I prefer football uniforms to this."

I looked at her. "Have you been talking to Chance again?"

She shrugged yet again and I rolled my eyes. She fully expected me to give her every detail of my love life while never wanting to reveal hers which was annoying. But she'd always been like that, not the giddy tell-all type, which I could respect.

"I think it's good. He's a nice guy and I don't think he did anything wrong," I shared.

"Whatever. You good or do you need me to stick around?" she asked.

Two more guys were on the mat now and had started wrestling but I was pretty sure they were the last match since there were no guys warming up anymore.

"I'm good. I'm gonna wait for him to come out and see what the plan is," I told her.

"Okay, text if you're not coming home."

"I will."

After she left, it wasn't five minutes later when Chance came and sat by me.

"What's up?" he asked.

"Nothing. What's up with you? Are you guys getting back together?" I looked optimistically at him.

"I don't know. She's still accusing me of shit but at least I've got her talking now." He sighed. Poor guy. I knew Sharee could be a tough nut to crack at times.

"She'll come around," I offered.

"We'll see. What're you doing here?"

I felt my face flush before telling him, "I came to watch someone."

"Yeah? Who?"

"Ryker Powers."

He looked at me in surprise. "Really?"

About that time the last match ended and the teams went out to shake hands before heading to their respective locker rooms.

I frowned. "Yes?"

"Oh, well, it's just that I already told you he's a, uh, he's kind of a…"

"Player?"

He acted relieved that I'd been the one to say it. "Yeah. So what's a nice girl like you doing with him?"

"He's a nice guy."

He choked on the soda he'd taken a drink of then gave me a look all, seriously?

I frowned some more. "He is. I mean, I know he was a manwhore, but we've been spending time together."

"Just be careful is all I can tell you."

"Hey, do you know who that blonde was who ran out to hug him?" I really wanted to know who the hell she was.

"Nikki Clark."

I glanced over at him. "And she would be…"

He lifted a shoulder. "All I know is she's what they call a Ring Rat but she and Powers have been hooking up for years from what I've heard." At the look on my face, he backtracked. "I mean, I could be wrong. I'm just telling you what I've heard is all."

"Hm."

Some guy hollered, "Hey, Reynolds! You coming?" then and Chance held a hand up to him to wait.

"I've gotta go. We're hitting a party over at Luke Warner's. You should come if you can. And if you can get Sharee there, that'd be good too. Good seeing you, Frankie. And like I said, just be careful with Powers." He put his arm around me and gave me a brotherly hug while I frowned again.

The stands were clearing out so I went down and stood against the wall waiting for Ryker to come out and texting Sharee while I waited letting her know I'd talked to Chance. I told her about the party and she actually seemed interested which shocked me. I texted that I'd ask Ryker if he wanted to go, and if so, we could meet her there or something. She responded with a "K" and as I was putting my phone in my purse, I looked up to see Ryker coming out dressed in jeans and another of his many hoodies. I pushed off the wall to go to him but stopped when I saw Blondie/Nikki talking to him. Good grief.

I waited where I was and was not too happy when I watched her hug him and he hugged her back. Nor was I thrilled when she kissed his cheek then giggled as she wiped the lipstick off. And that's when his eyes hit mine and I saw surprise and maybe a bit of fear in his but I wasn't sure.

Okay, I had two choices here. I could turn and leave before he even got to me, ending it between us then and there because I was jealous. Or I could stay and let the past be the past (hopefully, Nikki was his past) and be an adult and congratulate him on his win then ask him about her later.

I actually came up with an option one-point-oh which was to charge him, knocking him down in the process, then commence to beating the shit out of him for flirting with another woman. Since he'd be tired from the match I could probably get in a few good punches before running away unscathed. I thought this wasn't a half bad idea.

But before I could put any of my ideas into action, he'd walked to me, his hair messy probably from Nikki running her fingers through it, and said, "Hey."

"Hey," I returned forcing a smile. "Great job!"

"Thanks. And thanks for coming."

"You're welcome. I'm glad you won."

"Yeah."

He took my elbow leading me to go with him as he started walking. Once outside the gym, instead of going straight out the front lobby, he turned left, heading down a long hallway probably to the back parking lot.

"That was exciting!" I exclaimed trying to lighten the mood.

I got a "Meh" sound as a response.

"So, I don't understand how you won. I mean, not that you weren't better because you were. It's just that the score was tied then right at the end, you got a point."

"It's hard to explain."

"Okay. I mean, I heard the announcer say something about riding time but I don't' understand that."

"I don't really wanna talk about it right now," he mumbled.

"Oh. Well, I was just trying to figure out where that extra point came from and how things were scored," I pointed out.

Suddenly his fist went out to the side and hit a metal utility room door making a really loud noise and causing me to jump two feet in the air. "I said I don't wanna fuckin' talk about it!" he yelled as he walked ahead of me.

Good lord.

"O-okay. Sorry," I squeaked out from behind him, stopping because I was just going to turn around and go back to the lobby because I'd parked out front.

But just as I turned to head back, he grabbed me by the arm, spinning me back to face him. "Where're you going?" snapped.

I motioned behind me with my thumb. "I'm parked out front so I thought I'd go out that way. You're not in the greatest of moods, so I thought I'd—"

"Thought you'd what? Go meet Chance Reynolds at Luke's party?" His eyes were hard on mine, cold, as he waited for me to respond.

What the hell? Had he taken steroids before the match and now he was having some kind of roid rage?

"Well, yeah, I mean, I was gonna ask you if you wanted to go to the party but Chance is just a friend, so…"

"I'll just bet he is."

"Hey, no need to be a jerk. I could say the same thing about your dancer girlfriend."

Oh, damn. Here we went again.

He raised his eyebrows and snorted. "That never meant anything," he answered cruelly.

God. He was being such a jerk. Would he be saying that about me to someone someday?

And now my eyes were watering.

"Are you saying you never even cared about her? You're a real prick, you know that?" I choked on a sob. "Call me when you're back to yourself, Ryker." I turned to go and got maybe one step away from him when he came in from behind wrapping his arms around me and pulling my back against his front.

"I'm sorry, Francesca," he whispered in my ear. I could feel his heart pounding against my back. "I told you we needed to talk, that there were rules."

I tried getting out of his grasp but he wasn't budging. "I don't know if I want to follow your rules," I admitted.

His body went slack against mine signaling disappointment? Resignation?

"I need to go," I whispered.

His arms got tighter as his body went rigid. "Stay," he said softly. My head fell back against his chest and I let out a breath. "Please."

I turned in his arms and looked up meeting eyes that were full of supplication.

"Let me go to my car and I'll follow you," I suggested.

He nodded then leaned down to touch his lips to mine. "I'll drive around. Wait for me."

I nodded back then walked in the opposite direction.

If he were anyone else, I'd have told him to bite me. But I cared about him, having fallen so hard for him in the three weeks we'd known each other, which was crazy, but the heart wants what the heart wants and what're you gonna do?

I waited for Ryker and when I saw his car, I backed out and followed him to his house.

As I drove, I thought about how I really didn't know him at all. He'd been so fun this week with the kids, had seemed to lighten up so much, and then tonight happened. He'd won his match but obviously hadn't been happy about it. Since I'd never watched him wrestle before, maybe in his mind he felt he'd performed poorly and was pissed about it even though I thought he'd done great. I know I was always in a bad mood after a game when I hadn't played well and didn't want to talk about it for a while but I never took my anger out on anyone. Maybe it was a guy thing, aka, ego thing and he was embarrassed that I'd seen him on a bad night.

Lots of questions to be answered.

When we got to his neighborhood, I'd decided that tonight would either make or break us and the truth finally needed to be told. I had to know where things were going with us and if we couldn't work through this together, there was no need to continue.

And I was completely terrified.

At his house he pulled into the drive next to the blue truck I'd hidden behind the day I went to ask him out and saw him with VW Bug girl. I parked on the street and watched him jog to me as soon as he got out of his car, meeting me at my door.

"Hey," he said, taking my hand and walking toward the house. He brought my hand to his mouth kissing the back of it, keeping it at his mouth as we went.

I was still in my head about everything and didn't respond.

Once inside the house, I heard a guy holler from the kitchen, "Nice job, bro! Crawford's no longer undefeated!"

"Yeah," Ryker answered as he took my coat and hung it on the coat rack. He looked down at me. "I'm gonna go take a shower." At my alarmed expression, you know, at the fact that he was going to leave me alone with whoever was in the kitchen, he explained. "It's just Loch. Lemme get you a beer while you wait. Okay?"

Crap. This whole night was just shit. But trying to be a good sport I whispered, "Okay," and followed him into the kitchen sitting on the barstool he pulled out for me.

"Hey, Frankie!" Loch turned and said from where he stood at the stove cooking something.

"Hi," I answered with a smile.

"Here." Ryker handed me a beer bottle. "I'll be back." He leaned down and gave me a sweet kiss then left the room.

"So, I'm making a chicken quesadilla. You want one?" Loch asked.

"No, thanks. I already ate dinner."

He shrugged. "I've got plenty of stuff. I'm making Ryke one too 'cause he's always starving after matches."

"That's okay. But I can help if you want me to," I said, getting off the stool.

"Definitely. There's a green pepper and onion in the fridge if you don't mind getting them out. Cutting board's over there," he nodded his head to the right. "Knives are in the block."

I opened the refrigerator and found the vegetables then after washing them in the sink, went to the cutting board to chop.

"What'd you think of the match?" Loch questioned.

I shrugged. "I didn't understand the scoring much."

"Yeah, you kinda have to know what's going on to get it. Ryke can explain it, though."

I huffed out a humorless laugh. "Already tried that approach and got yelled at," I murmured mostly to myself.

"Hey," Loch called. When I looked over at him, he stated, "He's always in a bad mood after a close match. To be honest, I didn't think he'd win this one. That Crawford guy's a beast." He turned back to the skillet and flipped the quesadilla. "I wrestled a couple years in high school and it takes a lot out of you. Most of the time you're physically and mentally wasted. Not getting to eat what you want, hungry all the fuckin' time. It definitely takes a toll. That's why I cut him slack most of the time."

"I know it's a tough sport. Probably the toughest, actually," I agreed, cutting up the last of the onion. I carried the cutting board over and set it on the counter next to him. "All done. Anything else?"

"Nope. I've got the other stuff here, thanks."

I walked to the bar and picked up my beer and went back and leaned a hip on the counter near Loch. "So, he's always in a bad mood after?"

"Not always. Just depends if he won and sometimes how he won. He's just very hard on himself." He thought for a second and looked at me. "Why? Was he a dick tonight?" I shrugged before taking a drink. "I know this is gonna sound strange, but he's got an agenda. And when he strays from it, he tends to get a little pissy." At my questioning look, he said, "Since he's not a big sharer, I'm not sure he'll explain it to you. But you gotta know, Ryker sees things as black or white. There's no gray area. And once he's focused on something, he's gonna get it no matter what or die trying."

"Oh." Was I on his agenda? If not, was I going to get in the way?

Loch used the spatula to place the quesadilla on a plate then used a pizza cutter to cut it into slices. Next he sprayed PAM on the skillet and placed another tortilla in it then added the chicken, veggies and cheese and covered it all with another tortilla.

"But he's pretty simple to figure out. That's what I was trying to say at the party the other night." He turned to me. "You're in his sights, he wants you, he's gonna make it happen." He winked at me and turned back to the stove, flipping the tortillas.

"What if I don't want it to happen?"

He snorted. "Another thing I tried telling you at the party? He's mentioned you a couple times and he never talks about women to anyone. Ever. Also, he hasn't seen anyone else for going on three weeks now. Isn't that about the time you guys met?"

"I believe so," I answered. Well, that was at least some good news.

"What I'm saying is, if you don't want it to happen, you need to let him know because he won't stop until he's got you."

"Can I ask you something?"

"Shoot."

"Has he always been this intense?"

He chuckled. "Pretty much. When we were little, maybe about nine and ten, our dad started teaching us about car engines. Dad's a mechanic and owns a garage with our uncle. Anyway, Dad had a disassembled car engine in our garage at home that he showed us one Saturday morning and told us to put it back together. There was one of those big tool chests in there and Dad said to have at it. I laughed and ran off to play, but Ryker spent the entire day putting the engine back together, skipping lunch and dinner until Dad finally had to go out and get him at, like, eleven o'clock that night. Dad said when he went in the garage Ryker was just screwing in the oil filter adaptor which is the last part. So you see what I mean?"

I nodded. That *was* pretty intense especially for a ten year old.

"I mean, he's a good guy and likes to have fun too, but ever since... well, since the end of his freshman year at Hallervan, he's stayed pretty focused. He's set a goal for himself and he's intent on reaching it. I think his collegiate record now is something like one-hundred-fifteen wins and twenty-four losses which is definitely badass. Most of those losses came his freshman year when he was competing against seniors. His goal is to go undefeated this year."

"What kinda shit are you feeding her?" Ryker remarked as he walked into the kitchen wearing a gray Hallervan t-shirt and jeans. He was barefooted and his hair was still wet and he looked good enough to eat. Dang. He stopped at the fridge and pulled out a beer for himself raising an eyebrow at me to see if I wanted another. I shook my head so he closed the door then came to stand by me kissing me on the forehead when he got there. Now this was the Ryker I'd fallen for and I felt myself beginning to relax a tiny bit. He twisted the cap off his beer, throwing it in the trash and took a swig before pointing the bottle at the pan Loch was using. "That for me?"

"The one on the plate is," Loch told him jerking his head toward the already-cooked quesadilla.

"Thanks," Ryker said, picking up the plate. He first offered me a piece which I turned down and I swear, in less than a minute, he'd eaten the whole thing.

"Jesus. Hold out your fuckin' plate," Loch said, annoyed. When Ryker did as told, Loch put the second quesadilla on it. "See how spoiled he is?" Loch commented to me.

Ryker smirked then tore pieces off the thing and stuffed them in his mouth one by one, finishing the entire thing in about the same amount of time as he had the first one. Jeez.

"You think that's why you're in a bad mood because you're hungry?" I blurted without thinking.

Loch barked out a laugh. "That's what my girlfriend says." He looked at his brother. "They don't realize how much you *do* eat, which is a shit ton, so what *is* your reason for being an asshole tonight?"

I choked on my beer knowing Ryker probably thought I'd complained to Loch about how he'd behaved, which I had in a roundabout way, which didn't count, right?

Ryker put his plate in the dishwasher as he asked, "Really wanna know?"

I did. Yes, I *really* wanted to know.

I saw him look at Loch with a smirk because he was probably going to say something smartassed but then he glanced at me and I saw his expression turn serious. "I probably should've lost that match."

"Why?" Loch inquired.

Ryker's mood had soured right before my very eyes but he took in a breath and blew it out before explaining. "The last point came down to riding time. The timekeeper had me at a minute twenty five and Crawford at twenty-two seconds. Crawford's coach argued that their scorekeeper had him at twenty-seven which would've negated the point given." He shrugged a shoulder, an annoyed look on his face. "So according to them, we should've gone into overtime. That would've happened, I would've lost for sure. I was tired and he had me on the ropes."

Although I was so happy that he'd opened up and been truthful, I frowned. "So what?" He turned his head to me, his expression bordering on pissed off. "The official timekeeper said you won the point. Who cares what that coach said? Of course he's gonna fight for his player and say the time was wrong. According to the books, it wasn't. Accept it and move on."

I'd watched Ryker's expression turn soft as I talked. Good. He got it.

He looked at Loch. "Now you know why I keep her around."

I rolled my eyes at Loch who was grinning. Then I let out a yelp when Ryker scooped me up and carried me bridal style out of the kitchen.

"I'll be at Simone's tonight," Loch yelled after us.

"Good!" Ryker hollered back. He looked at me as he opened his bedroom door. "That means you can be as loud as you want tonight."

He laughed when I smacked him in the chest after he set me down. He cradled my face in his hands before saying, "God, I really like you." Then he gave me a knee-buckling kiss.

Well, it was official. I was the idiot in love with someone who really liked me. Yay.

When he started to pull my shirt over my head, I stopped him. "We need to have that talk, Ryker. And I want to know about these rules of yours."

I saw his jaw muscles jump as he looked down at me. "You wanna talk. Now."

I nodded as I sat on his bed, patting the spot next to me for him to sit but he turned and grabbed the chair at his desk, turning it to sit in it backward across from me.

"So talk," he prompted irritably.

Uh, not going the way I wanted it to. I guessed he'd shared enough earlier to last him another six months but whatever.

"Okay, well, first of all, tell me you cared about Nikki."

He took a deep breath and blew it out. "I still do. She's a good friend."

That was good albeit somewhat hard to take. But I was glad he'd shared.

"Okay, other than the obvious, I wanna know why you're so intent on winning every match this year?"

You'd have thought I'd called his mother a bad name by the way he looked at me.

"Next question."

Really?

I bit my lip as I stared at him. "What happened your freshman year that's made you feel like you have to win?"

He narrowed his eyes. "What the fuck did Loch tell you?"

"Not a lot but he alluded to the fact that something happened freshman year that's pushed you."

"Next."

Was he kidding?

"We're not gonna get anywhere if you won't answer," I said.

"Why the fuck do we need to talk to begin with? I mean, this really isn't any of your business."

Wow.

"Well, that's another question I have. Why do you get so nasty when you're uncomfortable? God. You can go from zero to jerk in one-point-five seconds." I stood up ready to leave.

He stretched his legs out knowing I was getting ready to bolt and they'd hinder me as he crossed his strong arms over his muscled chest. I put my hands on my hips and we had a stare down until I broke it.

"Look, if you don't want to tell me anything, that's fine. You're the one who brought it up saying there were rules and we needed to talk." For the second time tonight tears filled my eyes. "But if we can't get past this, I—I don't see any reason for us to continue seeing each other." I saw his eyes get dark at hearing this. And now, time for the truth which would make or break us. "I want a relationship with you, Ryker. If all I wanted was a fuck buddy, then what we have would work just fine." I swallowed roughly. "But I want to *know* you. I love you."

He stood so fast his chair went flying backward. "No." He looked as if I'd struck him as he shook his head looking everywhere but at me. A moment later, he rubbed his hands over his face and finally looking me in the eye said, "I can't do this right now, Francesca. I just can't."

"Wh-what?" The tears were free falling down my face now.

"I'm sorry."

He left the room leaving me standing there in shock. A few minutes later after getting myself together, I walked into the living room, grabbed my coat from the rack and left.

I drove home in a daze totally on autopilot.

When I pulled into the complex I sat in my car for a few minutes staring out the windshield at nothing.

Well, I'd done it. I'd pushed Ryker knowing things could go badly, and boy, had they ever.

When another car pulled in, it jolted me into reality and I finally got out of my car to go inside my apartment.

"Francesca! What's the matter, honey? Why are you crying?" Mrs. B asked from her balcony.

Huh. I hadn't even realized I was still crying.

I gazed up at her concerned face. "It's over."

"Oh, sweetie, you get on up here right this minute."

I numbly walked to the stairs and up where Mrs. B was waiting on me at her door.

"Come on in, child. Let me fix you some tea even though it's late and the caffeine will keep me up. But this is definitely a time for tea."

I went in and sat down at the kitchen table watching as she filled the kettle with water and placed it on the stovetop then got out cups, saucers and teabags. She busied herself around the kitchen setting the cups and saucers on the table and getting out ladyfingers arranged them on a plate that she also set on the table. When the tea kettle whistled, she turned off the burner and carried it over setting it on a trivet in the middle of the table.

"That's more of the apple cinnamon tea. Go ahead and pour your water," she prodded seeing that I was out of it. She even placed two ladyfingers on my saucer since I probably wouldn't have had the wherewithal to do so.

I poured water in my cup and held onto the string of the teabag dipping it up and down in the water.

"Women are like teabags, you know. Eleanor Roosevelt herself said so."

This caught my attention and I glanced at Mrs. B waiting for her to go on.

"Uh huh. Mrs. Roosevelt said you never know how strong it is until it's placed in hot water."

I nodded absentmindedly.

"And that's how we women are, isn't it, Francesca? We're strong. We can handle anything because we're tough, right?"

Another noncommittal nod.

I watched as Mrs. B stood from the table and went back into the kitchen. She pulled a glass from the cabinet and filled it with water then walked back to the table and tossed the water right in my face.

"What're you doing?" I shrieked, standing up and sputtering.

"I thought that'd do it. Here." She gave me a hand towel and I wiped my face throwing in a few glares at her as if she was nuts. "Now. Have a seat and tell me what happened."

I sat down and started at the beginning telling her how I'd dreamed of marrying Ryker but feared I'd spoiled things by sleeping with him, I explained how I'd taken her advice and we'd become friends as well as lovers, and finished up with my disoriented drive home.

She'd sat quietly listening intently to my story, nodding, smiling or frowning at all the right places and when I finished, she again nodded before taking a sip of tea.

"So?" I asked.

"So," she answered in a sigh.

"I'm an idiot, aren't I? I did everything wrong and that's why I'll never have a Marco who I'll be with for fifty-four years. I'm gonna die an old maid."

Oh, yay. More tears.

She handed me a napkin and I wiped my eyes. "I told him I loved him and he walked out on me."

She nodded.

"And now it's over."

She picked up a ladyfinger and took a bite humming in satisfaction at the taste of it.

I stared at her for a moment before asking, "Don't you have anything to say?"

She smiled sweetly at me.

I looked down at my cup trying to stop more tears from coming which didn't help in the least. "See? It's so bad even you don't know how to fix it this time." I gazed up at her through puffy eyes to see her electric blue ones full of sympathy. "I wish you'd talk. But if you did, you'd probably just tell me again that I needed to play it smart if I want his eyes to open. You'd say to go back to being his friend and it'll all work out. Well, you know what, Mrs. B? I already tried that and it blew up in my face!"

"Tell me why it blew up."

Oh, now she wanted to talk. Ugh.

"Because I pushed. I wanted something so badly that I went for it and look what it got me. A big steaming bowl of nothing."

She leaned back in her chair. "Francesca, have you ever thought that sometimes people need to be pushed?"

I sank back in my chair my posture horrible as I scowled at her. What was with all her cryptic mumbo jumbo?

"I pushed him and he pushed away. End of story. Thanks for playing, try again!" I stated sarcastically.

"I want you to follow what you just told me then let me know how it goes."

I shook my head and stood carrying my cup and saucer to the sink. "Thank you for the tea. I'll be by Saturday to get your grocery list."

~*~*~*~

While I'd been at Mrs. B's, Sharee had texted that she was going to Luke's party with Ciara and Madison which was good because I didn't want to explain why I was crying. It was also good because when I showered, I sobbed loudly and didn't have to worry about her hearing.

It was only a little after nine when I crawled into bed. I was exhausted from all the crying and needed a break from the world. Which was when my phone chimed.

Text Message—Thurs, Jan 29, 9:06 p.m.

Ree: Ryker's here, where are you?

Oh, good. I'd be willing to bet my left eyeball that Nikki was there too and they were going to hook up.

Text Message—Thurs, Jan 29, 9:06 p.m.

Me: In bed

Text Message—Thurs, Jan 29, 9:07 p.m.

Ree: What? Why?

Text Message—Thurs, Jan 29, 9:07 p.m.

Me: Long story

Text Message—Thurs, Jan 29, 9:07 p.m.

Ree: Did you two have a fight?

Text Message—Thurs, Jan 29, 9:08 p.m.

Me: It's over

Text Message—Thurs, Jan 29, 9:08 p.m.

Ree: I'm sorry. What'd you fight about?

Might as well get it over with.

Text Message—Thurs, Jan 29, 9:09 p.m.

Me: He was a jerk after his match. I almost left but stupid me had to follow him home. Loch was there. We talked a little then Ryker & I went to talk except all he wanted to do was fuck. He wouldn't answer my questions. I told him I loved him. He said he couldn't do this and I left.

Text Message—Thurs, Jan 29, 9:10 p.m.

Ree: Wow. I'm so sorry, Frankie : (

Text Message—Thurs, Jan 29, 9:10 p.m.

Me: Me too

Text Message—Thurs, Jan 29, 9:10 p.m.

Ree: Blonde chick is here hanging on him

Something in me clicked when I read her text. I'd been chasing Ryker from the start and although I was in love with him, I was finished chasing him. If he wanted Nikki, then I wished them luck but I thought it was sad that he felt that all he needed in his life was hookups. It dawned on me that he and I lived in two totally different worlds and never the twain shall meet, as Mrs. B would say. And I was fine with that.

Text Message—Thurs, Jan 29, 9:11 p.m.

Me: Good for them. I'm going to sleep. Love you. Be careful (I know I didn't ask about Chance & I'm sorry. Tell me about him tomorrow, k?) xo

Text Message—Thurs, Jan 29, 9:14 p.m.

Ree: I will. Love you too xx

I turned off my light, rolled to my side and was out.

~*~*~*~

Even though I was okay, I called in sick to school Friday morning not ready to face Ryker just yet.

I was sure he'd been with Nikki and I didn't want to see the smug look on his face when he came in.

So I went back to sleep.

Share woke me at two asking if I was going to get out of bed today. I told her I'd get up whenever I wanted to. She informed me that Ryker hadn't left the party with Nikki and I told her I didn't care and went back to sleep.

At seven, Mom called asking if I was coming to dinner. I lied and told her I didn't feel well and after we hung up, I slept.

At ten Saturday morning, I finally got up and showered after having spent over thirty-six hours in bed. I changed my sheets, put in a load of laundry then called to set up a nail appointment for Sharee and me that afternoon. That evening, she and I went to a movie after eating at a new restaurant we'd been wanting to try out.

She'd told me that she'd talked to Chance at the party but wasn't sure she wanted to start things up again her reason being that since he was pre-med and she was pre-law they'd never see each other anyway. It made sense but I was still sad. I guess the dreamer in me wanted them to be together and happy, and thinking that way actually surprised me because I knew that what had happened with Ryker and me hadn't broken me. I was still a dreamer and that was a good thing.

Sunday morning I cleaned around the house, vacuuming, dusting, and mopping floors before grabbing my Kindle and getting lost in *Jane Eyre* well into the evening. Only then did I think about lesson plans and having to face Ryker but I knew I'd be okay. If Jane Eyre could make it through everything she had, I could deal with one.

~*~*~*~

"Where were ya Friday, kid?" Coach G asked Monday morning when I got to the gym.

Ryker was already there setting up two volleyball nets and I saw his lips purse when I told Coach that I must've picked up a nasty bug the night before.

The first graders came running in right after the bell.

"Where were you Friday, Coach M?" Taylor, a cute little snowy-haired girl asked.

"I was sick," I explained.

"Did you go to the doctor?" Jeffery, a Precious Moments figurine lookalike asked.

"No, but I did stay in bed for a very long time."

"I'm glad you're back," Melody, the resident fashion plate in training, said and I gave her a hug thanking her.

"You should've been here, Coach M! We played dodgeball against Coach Powers by himself and we won! Jonathan hit him really hard in the head too!" Jeffery informed me with his big brown eyes sparkling.

"Oh no!" I said and looked at Jonathan who was bigger than the rest of the kids but shy as all get out. "Did you knock any sense into him?" Jonathan blushed as he gave me a shrug and the rest of the kids giggled like crazy asking Coach Powers if he'd heard what I said.

With his back to us all hooking up the net he replied, "I heard it. And you can tell Coach M that I think maybe it did." He looked over his shoulder at me and winked.

Now what was that all about?

"Okay, are you ready to pick teams?" I asked and chaos ensued when twenty-two little wriggly bodies began jumping all over the place. "Raisa and Marshall, you're the team captains for this side of the floor and Jackie and Gerald, you're the team captains for this side and you get to pick whomever you want to be on your teams."

I always made sure to pick kids who'd generally be chosen last to be the captains that way they'd be guaranteed to be on a good team and maybe it helped their self-esteem a little.

The nets were finished and the games began. Ryker and I walked around showing the kids how to serve underhanded, of course letting them scoot up if they couldn't get the ball over the net and teaching them how the game was scored.

When the bigger kids came in, the nets were raised and teams picked. They were a bit more serious about the game and knew what they were doing so it didn't take a whole lot of coaching them.

Ryker didn't say another word to me the rest of the day only waving when he left for practice at lunch.

The next two weeks went the same. Ryker's and my lesson plans being checked by Coach G then used to pick different activities to get the kids moving and Ryker remaining silent and aloof toward me but having fun with the kids which I was glad of. They loved when he got involved and I had to admit it was quite entertaining to see. He also missed a couple days for matches, and glutton for punishment that I was, I couldn't help checking the school paper to keep up with how he was doing. He was still undefeated for the year, which made me happy for him.

So even though I was still hurt I felt like I was slowly healing. Nothing like having to see the object of your pain on a daily basis to speed up the old healing process. Good to see that my use of sarcasm was in no way affected by everything.

Valentine's Day came and went. It was on a Saturday and Ryker had had a match the Friday before, so at least I didn't have to suffer through seeing him getting sent a cheesy stuffed teddy bear or some stupid box of candy from whichever flavor of the week he was seeing. Since we were both single, Sharee and I decided to make the most of the annoying-only-if-you're-single holiday by making a reservation at a very posh restaurant. We'd noticed that everyone from the maître d' to our waiter had treated us as if we were a couple which had us giggling the whole time. We even called Gladys and put her on speaker phone so she could hear when Sharee stood up at our table in the middle of dinner holding up her glass of champagne and shouted, "She said yes!" and we all three laughed like crazy when the other patrons clapped for us.

The strangest thing that happened was the Monday after VD when Sharee and I met at O'Leary's after our classes for drinks to celebrate our coupledom which had become our running joke. I got to the bar first and needed something a little harder than usual and ordered a scotch on the rocks with a splash of club soda. Just after taking my first sip and letting out a sigh, I heard someone call my name. Looking up, I saw Loch standing at my table smiling down at me with a lovely auburn-haired woman at his side.

"Hey, Loch," I said smiling back at him.

"Hey, Frankie. This is my girlfriend Simone St. John. Simone, this is Frankie Mangenelli."

She and I said our hellos then Loch whispered something in her ear. She smiled telling me it was nice meeting me then she went to a table where another couple was sitting.

"Would you like to sit down?" I asked Loch.

"Sure."

"So, how've you been?" I inquired, taking another much-needed sip of my drink.

"I've been good. You?"

I shrugged giving him a weak smile. "Could be better, could be worse."

"Frankie, I'm just gonna throw this out there but I want you to know that Ryker's completely miserable."

I tapped my glass with my fingernail hating that I liked hearing that. "Well, I'm sure his latest fling will help make him feel better."

"He hasn't seen anyone since you."

I huffed out a laugh as I looked at him. "Sure he hasn't. We both know you're brother's not the most discriminating person when it comes to whomever he takes to bed. Matter of fact, I heard he was with Nikki the night he and I split up."

He shook his head. "Nikki hasn't been over in months."

I raised my eyebrows. "But that doesn't mean he hasn't gone to her."

He shook his head again. "Look. I know he's known to be a huge player, but honestly, he's not as bad as people make him out to be. Now, my brother Gable? Different story. But you know Ryker. He doesn't let people in very easily. So, yeah, over the past four years, he may have been with five, six different women but it was never anything serious until you."

"What're you trying to tell me, Loch? That I should run back into his arms because he's been abstinent for three weeks?"

He chuckled. "I just wanted you to know he's been the broodiest son of a bitch since you two stopped seeing each other. Even more so than usual. I might be telling you to take his ass back so I can get some relief from all the bitchiness he's been throwing my way."

"Hey!" Sharee said walking up to the table. "I know you." She smiled at Loch who stood and shook her hand.

"How are you?" he asked as she sat but he remained standing.

"I'm doing great, thank you. You?" she asked.

"Doing great as well. I'll let you two do your thing. It was good seeing you both again." He looked at me. "Help a guy out, would you?" He winked before walking away.

Sharee looked at me curiously. "What was that all about?"

I rolled my eyes. "Apparently, Ryker's been miserable since we broke up and hasn't been the easiest to live with."

"Oohh, that's good, right?"

"Depends on how you look at it, I guess."

"You know, I'm just gonna say it." She gave me a pointed look. "I know you think you've handled things pretty well, and for the most part you have, but, Frankie, you've been miserable too. Don't think I haven't heard you crying in the shower."

My mouth dropped open. "You have? I mean, no you haven't! I'm doing fine!"

"I'll have what she's having," she said to the waitress who'd stopped at the table. "Lagavulin 16?" she asked and at my nod the waitress smiled then went to put in her order. "It's okay. I know you fell hard for him. But who's to say he's not been doing some heavy thinking since your split?"

I took another drink wincing a bit at the burn in my throat. "He's shown no sign of being miserable to me. You should see him in class, getting crazy with the kids. You should've seen him the other day when he chased the first graders around the gym acting like some damned monkey." I giggled in spite of myself remembering how ridiculous he'd been.

"Of course he's shown no signs. He's happiest when he's with you, don't you see that?" The waitress set Sharee's drink down in front of her, and Sharee thanked her, picking it up and taking a long pull on it. "God, I needed that. Jurisprudence just about put me to sleep tonight."

"So are you saying we should get back together?"

"That's up to you two. You still love him. If he's willing to finally talk, who knows? You may get things worked out."

"Thanks a lot. I'd just settled into the fact that he and I were over and I needed to move on and now you and Loch are making me feel things again. The only thing I've felt in weeks is this scotch at the back of my throat and now you've ruined that."

She laughed. "Welcome back to the human race where *feelings* screw you the fuck up. Just remember, though, if it doesn't work out with you two, you always have me to come back to, lover." She batted her eyelashes at me.

I laughed with her. "God, we're pathetic. We need boyfriends STAT."

~*~*~*~

That night just as I was falling asleep, my phone chimed. I picked it up squinting at it in the dark.

Text Message—Mon, Feb 16, 11:23 p.m.

Ryker: I hope you had a good day today. See you tomorrow xx

I'd changed his name on Sunday after my Jane Eyre-athon because I'd thought the other name had been stupid. And I didn't need a reminder anymore to be his friend.

But the text was a surprise. Then I remembered and thought that Loch had probably told him he'd seen me at O'Leary's. Whatever.

But I read the message with a small smile before deleting it.

~*~*~*~

The next day, things at PE had been the usual until lunch.

I'd gone into Coach G's office as usual to eat while sitting on his couch and watching his little TV until the bell rang, assuming Ryker had already left for practice. I'd just popped my cup of noodles into the microwave when I heard a sound at the door. Turning to the right, I saw Ryker standing in the doorway.

"Oh! I thought you already left for practice," I said.

God. He was bigger than life, his presence filling up the entire doorway to where I saw nothing but him.

When he still stood there just looking at me, I wasn't sure what to do. "What?" I finally asked.

"I miss you."

Damn it. Direct hit to the heart.

I bit my lip not knowing what to do. I wanted to tell him I missed him too and couldn't we try again but I was still confused about everything, so the only thing that came out was, "I'm not sure what to say."

I saw his eyes flare for a second then he nodded and left.

The microwave beeped and I pulled my noodles out then sat on the couch halfway watching a guy on *Maury* confess that he'd slept with his wife's three sisters. Jesus. And I thought I had it bad.

~*~*~*~

That night just before I turned out my light, my phone chimed.

Text Message—Tues, Feb 17, 11:07 p.m.

Ryker: Goodnight, beautiful

I smiled right before deleting the text.

~*~*~*~

The next day at school went as well as the day before. The kids were enthusiastic to play kickball and had a blast. When Ryker left that day, he'd made sure to put his hand on the small of my back and tell me goodbye.

That night in my athletic injury class, the guest speakers were coming in to talk about their injuries and treatment they'd received. Jared Littleson who was a linebacker for Hallervan's football team talked first telling us how he'd separated his ribs in a game when he'd made a tackle. He'd been out for two months and said the doctor told him he'd have been better off fracturing a rib instead because it would've healed faster. He'd had to be taped the first month constantly and he told us it hurt like a bitch when he had to sneeze.

Coach Nolan then demonstrated on Jared how to tape that type of injury. When he finished, he thanked Jared and looked at his notepad then around the room for a second.

"Frankie? Can you run across to the fieldhouse and see if Chance Reynolds is in the weight room by any chance? He's supposed to talk to us about turf toe."

"Sure, Coach," I said and left the room, jogging over to the fieldhouse that held the Athletic Director's office along with locker rooms for football, baseball and wrestling and of course had a weight room.

Once inside, I jogged down the hallway to the sound of rock music blaring and weights clanking. Once at the weight room, I stuck my head in to see several guys lifting.

"Hey, is Chance Reynolds in here?" I called.

Fifteen sets of peepers turned to look at me but I only focused on the pair of light brown eyes that glittered back at me. Ryker stood there shirtless (God help me) wearing a long pair of maroon athletic shorts that hung low on his hips and he looked amazing, his whole body covered in a light mist of perspiration. Gah.

"Hey, Frankie," Chance called. "What's up?"

I couldn't take my eyes off of Ryker as I told Chance, "Coach Nolan said you're supposed to speak to our class tonight."

"Fuck, I forgot. Okay, I'll be right there," Chance said as he toweled off.

By this time, Ryker was making his way over to me checking out the black yoga pants I wore as he did. When he got to me he smirked and said, "You trying to make every one of us pop a fuckin' boner with those pants?"

I huffed out a laugh. "That was exactly my intention."

"Frankie?" Coach Kennison, the Athletic Director, called from behind me out in the hallway and I turned to see what he needed.

"Yeah, Coach?"

At the same time I heard Ryker mumble, "Fuck me."

I looked over my shoulder to see him staring at my butt which embarrassed and thrilled me at the same time.

"You going back to the gym?"

"Yes."

"Think you can deliver a box to Coach Nolan for me?" Coach K asked.

"Sure. I'll be right there," I told him then wheeled around to see Ryker's eyes move slowly up my body to meet mine. "Enjoying the show?" I asked.

"Oh, fuck yeah. Your ass looks smokin' hot in those pants. Jesus fuck, Francesca," he mumbled.

I missed his calling me by my full name. Oh, hell, I missed him. But I still didn't think I was ready to move forward just yet.

I snorted and rolled my eyes. "Every girl on campus wears these, Ryker."

"Every girl doesn't have an ass like yours." He didn't even bother hiding the lust that flickered in his eyes.

"I've gotta get back to class," I said with a laugh shaking my head at him.

"Make sure to leave slowly," he replied, his amber eyes burning into mine revealing every dirty thought he was having right then.

I smacked his bare chest which was a mistake because it had me thinking my own dirty thoughts about him. Jeez. "See you tomorrow," I said, turning and leaving, conscious that his eyes were on my butt the entire time feeling mortified but also kind of loving it. I got the box from Coach K and delivered it to Coach Nolan then listened to Chance describing the debilitating effects of turf toe but a part of my brain was back at the weight room envisioning Ryker's magnificent body.

~*~*~*~

My phone chimed just as my head hit the pillow that night.

Text Message—Wed, Feb 18, 11:16 p.m.

Ryker: Don't tell me you're still wearing those pants because you might hear me trying to beat down your door in about 20 minutes

A moment later his next text came through.

Text Message—Wed, Feb 18, 11:16 p.m.

Ryker: G'night, gorgeous xx

I smiled as I looked at my phone and fell asleep with it in my hand.

~*~*~*~

Thursday we had the kids play freeze tag. Ryker jumped in and every time one of them tagged him, he "froze" in the silliest positions making the goofiest faces and the kids loved it. I cracked up on every one of them but his velociraptor took the cake. The look on his face was priceless along with the way he shortened his arms and held his hands as if they were claws. Coach G even got tickled on that one and laughed so hard he had a choking fit.

Before Ryker left that day he caught me in Coach G's office coming in and closing the door. "I just wanted to let you know I've got a match out of town tomorrow so I won't be here. But I also wanted to check something."

Nonplussed, I cocked my head to the side wondering what he had to check. Keeping his eyes on mine, he slowly stepped into me backing me against the wall then bending down, his lips a mere inch away from mine, he mumbled, "I just need to know," and he touched his mouth to mine.

What started out as an innocent little kiss gradually turned into something much hotter and definitely not innocent at all. By the end of it, one of my hands had slid up into his hair where my fingers twisted, tugging hard making a groan come from deep inside his throat. My other hand ended up on his shoulder, fingers digging in trying to pull him closer to me. As for him, his hand was in my hair, his fingers tangled in it clenching almost as hard as I was holding his, and his arm was wrapped tightly around my waist holding me as close to him as possible.

Dear God.

When he pulled away, we were both breathing hard, our eyes half-lidded and in no way hiding what we wanted from the other.

He nodded slowly as he looked down at me, his eyes aimed at my lips. "Yeah. I thought so." His eyes slid up to mine and he whispered, "Goodbye, Francesca," and left.

I stood against the wall for a moment, touching my fingers to my lips wondering if that had really just happened. The tingle in them let me know it had.

Apparently our chemistry was still on target. Damn.

~*~*~*~

That night, a text came in.

Text Message—Thurs, Feb 19, 11:22 p.m.

Ryker: I love your lips... I think mine buzzed for an hour afterward... I'll miss you tomorrow. 'Night xx

This time I wrote back.

Text Message—Thurs, Feb 19, 11:22 p.m.

Me: Have a safe trip and good luck tomorrow. P.S. my lips are still buzzing... I'll miss you too. Goodnight xo

Pretty sure I fell asleep with my fingers on my lips.

Friday, for some godforsaken reason, the first graders wanted to play dodgeball again. I truly didn't understand it. Maybe their exposure to violent video games had given them a thirst for blood. Whatever the reason, I couldn't say I was as happy to play as they were because after their begging me to join them, the minute I stepped out onto the playing field, I was nailed by twelve balls, all but two getting me in the head. Fun.

That night as I lay in bed, all I could think about was Ryker. I wondered if he'd won his match, wondered if he really missed me, wondered if we could be together and last.

And that's when my phone chimed and I smiled.

Text Message—Fri, Feb 20, 11:34 p.m.

Ryker: Hey, cara... you awake?

God, he could be so sweet.

Text Message—Fri, Feb 20, 11:34 p.m.

Me: Hi, handsome... I am...

Text Message—Fri, Feb 20, 11:34 p.m.

Ryker: How'd today go?

Text Message—Fri, Feb 20, 11:34 p.m.

Me: The bloodthirsty 1st graders chose dodgeball & talked me into playing. I think I have 12 knots on my head

Text Message—Fri, Feb 20, 11:35 p.m.

Ryker: Did they knock any sense into you? ;)

I chuckled.

Text Message—Fri, Feb 20, 11:35 p.m.

Me: Yeah, I think maybe they did ;) Did you win?

Text Message—Fri, Feb 20, 11:35 p.m.

Ryker: Good. I did. Finally got a fucking pin. It felt good.

Text Message—Fri, Feb 20, 11:36 p.m.

Me: Yay! Good for you! Congratulations!

Text Message—Fri, Feb 20, 11:36 p.m.

Ryker: Can I call you?

Text Message—Fri, Feb 20, 11:36 p.m.

Me: Yes

My phone rang five seconds later.

"Hey," I answered.

"Hey."

"Where are you?"

"Charter bus, just went through Portland."

"Dang. That's three more hours until you're home!"

"It'll be almost four hours total."

"Did you leave this morning?"

"No, we took off around one yesterday. Stayed overnight."

"Ah, okay. Well, at least you got rest last night before your match today, huh?"

"Yeah."

He sounded really tired.

"Are you able to sleep on the bus?" I asked.

"Not really. I've got my own seat but you know how it is. Even with the seat back, it's still not very comfortable."

Boy, did I know. Basketball is a long season and riding in busses and vans gets very tiresome very fast.

"Yeah."

"So…" I heard him cough nervously. "Are you, uh, doing anything tomorrow night?"

Tomorrow. Saturday. All I had planned was a whole lot of nothing. But should I tell him this making myself look like a loser or make something up pretending I was busy.

I decided I wasn't playing the game anymore and answered honestly.

"No, I'm not."

"Would you like to go to dinner with me? Maybe a movie afterward?"

I heard the quake in his voice. He was nervous and it was the cutest thing ever.

"I'd love to."

Hearing his huge sigh of relief had me biting my lips to keep from chuckling.

"Good," he said through his sigh.

"Yeah. Good."

"Francesca?"

"Yes?"

"I've missed you." His voice was deep and rumbly and I closed my eyes letting what he said flow over me.

"I've missed you too," I whispered.

"I was an idiot." I bit my lip. "You can agree," he said with a snort.

I chuckled. "Well, I won't disagree. How about that?"

"God. It's so good to be talking to you again," he said behind another sigh.

We talked for the rest of his trip, him telling me stories about him and his brothers growing up, me telling him about growing up in Texas then moving here and meeting Sharee and Gladys. We talked about our majors and what we wanted for our futures. I ultimately wanted to become an English professor either Hallervan or UDub but I wasn't going to be picky as long as it was somewhere I liked. He told me he wanted to coach wrestling at the collegiate level but didn't care where either as long as it was at a decent school.

We talked until the bus got into Seattle.

"I'll call you later and let you know what time I'm picking you up, okay?" he said.

"'Kay."

"Get some rest, baby. G'night."

"'Night, Ryker."

~*~*~*~

"Where are my strappy, black sandals?" I shrieked as I crawled around on the floor of my closet digging through too many pairs of shoes.

"My, my. Aren't we the nervous one?" Sharee asked from my doorway.

I sat back on my haunches and looked to see her swinging my shoes from her finger.

"I borrowed them a while back, remember?" She came into my room handing them to me then flopped on my bed. "That dress is hot!"

I turned and looked at the back in my wall mirror. "I'm not wearing a bra and I forgot to get a stick-on bra. You sure it's not too slutty?"

"That's what I like about it," she replied with a laugh. At my panicked look she laughed even more. "I'm just teasing. It's gorgeous. You're gorgeous. Ryker's gonna flip out when he sees you."

I checked the dress out again making sure she was right. It was a black bodycon dress I'd picked up when we'd gone shopping several weekends ago and I thought it was totally cute. It had a high neck in front, long sleeves and the hem hit me mid-thigh. But the draped open back that ended at my waist was what I loved. It was totally hot and made me feel sexy. Well, that and the thigh highs and lacy thong I was wearing.

I slipped on my sandals, buckling them at the side and looked in the mirror again.

"Perfect," Sharee shared. "Your makeup is great, all evening dramatic, and your hair's stunning with all the curls. Every man in the restaurant won't be able to keep his eyes off you."

"I'm only worried about one man," I mumbled, smoothing the dress down my thighs.

And speaking of, right then there was a knock on the door.

"I'll get it. You go do your lip gloss then you can have a grand entrance."

Eep!

I rushed to my bathroom as she left my room to get the door. As I applied more gloss, I heard her whistle and tell Ryker that he cleaned up nicely. With one last glance in the mirror, I blew out a breath then going through my room, I picked up the shiny black clutch I'd set out before going out to the living room.

Holy Mary on a motorcycle. The moment I laid eyes on Ryker, I stopped dead in my tracks. Dear sweet Jesus, he looked good. Black slacks, slate blue button up with a navy tie and black wingtip boots. Damn.

"You guys just gonna stare at each other all night or you going to dinner?" Sharee asked with a snort.

Ryker's eyes were all over me, moving from the toes of my strappy five-inch heels up to my hair then back down again. "You're stunning."

I smiled. "Thank you. You look hot!" I blurted and felt my face flush.

"You can say that again," Sharee murmured.

"Ready?" Ryker asked walking over to help me put on my black wool coat that hit just below my knees.

"I am," I said looping my arm through his.

"You guys have fun!" Sharee said as we headed out the door. "And make sure to do everything I'd do and then some," she called after me making me turn and scowl at her while Ryker chuckled.

He was driving a midnight blue sedan and held the door for me. "Who's car is this?" I asked.

"My mom's. I didn't think you'd want to try getting in and out of the Mustang in a dress since it's so low to the ground." He winked after helping me in then shut the door going around and getting in on the driver's side.

"Where are we going?"

"Mom and Dad told me about this Italian place, you do like Italian, right?"

"Ryker. What's my last name?" I said with a giggle.

"Oh, yeah," he answered with a snort. "So my parents recommended we order the tasting menu if you'd like that."

"That sounds great."

He kept looking at me as he drove making me squirm a bit in my seat, pulling my dress down at the thigh and adjusting the neckline until I finally looked at him and asked, "What?"

"Can't keep my eyes off you, Francesca. You're fucking beautiful."

"Thank you," I whispered shyly.

He reached over for my hand, bringing it up to brush his lips over the back of it before resting our clasped hands on his thigh.

I sighed in contentment finally feeling some peace after being so at odds with myself the past several weeks. Right then, driving to the restaurant, I knew that was where I was supposed to be at that very moment in time and with that very man.

The restaurant was the most romantic place I'd ever been. The tables all had a single curved booth, so we sat close together looking at our menus, mostly for the wine choices since we'd decided on the tasting menu. We settled on a very nice sauvignon blanc that would go well with the seafood we'd chosen.

As we waited for each course to come, we chatted comfortably about school, his wrestling, my basketball, the weather, how we thought the Mariners would do. The last made me laugh and I had to explain to him about the Mariners being my dad's fallback conversation when things got uncomfortable.

And in the midst of dinner, it suddenly came to me that Mrs. B had been right all along. Ryker and I had become friends after all, which had been the missing element at the beginning. I mean, I'd jumped in the sack with him without even knowing who he really was, and vice versa, so we'd gone about things backwards and had gotten hurt in the meantime. I'd pushed to know things that really weren't any of my business at that time because we hadn't known each other. I just hoped he'd feel comfortable enough to share with me now so that we could move forward.

"Holy fuck that's good," Ryker murmured as he tasted one of the five desserts that had been brought out.

I laughed because it all was seriously so good.

"Try this," he said, holding his fork out to me with the dessert he'd been eating on it.

I leaned over, opening my mouth and closing it over his fork and pulling back releasing his fork to taste what he was giving me.

I closed my eyes and moaned. "God, that *is* good." When he didn't say anything, I opened my eyes to see him staring at my mouth, his golden eyes glowing with lust.

His eyes slid up to hold mine as he put his hand on my thigh under the table, his fingers working to slowly move my dress up. When he got to the lace of my thigh high he groaned. "It's been pure fuckin' torture, I want you to know," he leaned down and whispered in my ear as his fingers flirted with the edge of my stocking.

"What has?" I whispered back.

"Seeing you every day and not being able to touch you."

Our waiter came to the table and I sat up quickly but Ryker kept his hand where it was, clutching my thigh hard because my movement had pushed me forward and his fingers were touching my center now. It took everything I had not to let out a moan when he glided a finger over me.

"Will there be anything else, sir?" the waiter asked.

Ryker looked at me, his finger still moving (gah!) and asked, "Is there anything else you need, baby?"

His eyes were hot on me as I answered, "No, I think we're finished here, thank you." I looked up at the waiter and smiled holding in a gasp when Ryker's finger slipped under the lacy fabric of my thong and he slid the tip inside me.

"I'll bring your check," the waiter said, giving a nod before leaving.

"Oh, my God," I breathed out. I moved a hand down and covered his, trying to pull it away from me. "Ryker, stop," I said under my breath.

"How wet are you for me, Francesca?" he whispered in my ear now circling his thumb on my clitoris.

Dear God. I could've come from his sexy voice alone. I closed my eyes and leaned against him, my breathing getting harder with each passing moment.

"If I dipped my fingers in, would I have something to lick off them?" he cajoled, his voice all gravelly.

Shit.

My breathing was heavy and my hand tightened on his. "Please," I begged him to stop.

He kissed the side of my head and removed his hand, pushing my dress down in the process. He clasped his hands on the table in front of him, his pointer finger staying up, then leaning forward slowly, he opened his mouth moving it down to take his finger inside it, dragging his teeth down to the first knuckle before closing his mouth around it and sucking on his way up.

I watched in fascination as he did this, the spasms in my womb making me clamp my legs together tightly as I tried fending off a damned orgasm.

He looked my way with a smirk knowing exactly what I was doing because my breathing had become erratic.

"Stop it!" I hissed through gritted teeth, my eyes pleading with him because I really didn't want to come in front of all these people and make a spectacle of myself. God!

He chuckled darkly and I socked him in the ribs making him grunt then laugh even harder.

"Just wait until I get you home," I threatened.

"Can't wait," he fired back as he pulled his wallet out of his inside jacket pocket and handed his credit card to the waiter who returned shortly with the receipt. Ryker signed then slid out of booth holding his hand out to help me. And we were out of there in a flash.

~*~*~*~

On the drive home, I got him back by reaching over and unzipping his slacks snaking a hand inside to stroke him.

What really got him was when I unbuckled my seatbelt and leaned over to take his length in my mouth.

"Ah, fuck me," he groaned as I rolled my tongue over his tip then sucking hard, moved my mouth down slowly as far as I could then did the same on the way up. "Francesca, stop," he ordered when we came to a stop. I kept going because he'd tortured me in the same delicious way and this was his payback. "I'm not fucking kidding. Stop now! My mom's coming toward the car."

Fuck.

Fuck!

I jerked my head up quickly watching as he tucked himself back in while I pretended to be looking at a spot on his tie.

He rolled his window down. "Hey, Ma. What's up?" he asked innocently.

"Just thought I'd drive the Mustang over so you didn't have to go all the way to the house," Mrs. Powers said.

"Good idea." Ryker looked at me and bugged out his eyes instantly making me huff out a laugh. "Let's get out, baby, and you can meet my ma."

Yay. Meeting the mother.

He rolled his window up, turning off the ignition then got out and came around to help me. His mom had walked around too, so as soon as I got out, she sucked in a breath and put her hands to her cheeks.

"Oh, my word! You're beautiful! You must be Francesca!" she said, moving in to grab me for a hug.

"Hello, Mrs. Powers," I replied, hugging her right back.

She pulled away still holding onto my forearms looking me over. Glancing at Ryker, she scolded, "She's so much prettier than you described!"

He'd talked about me to his mom? Wow.

"Hard to describe this kinda beauty, Ma."

And now I was blushing at being the center of attention.

"Thank you. And you're gorgeous, Mrs. Powers." And she was. I wasn't saying that to suck up to her. She had the same golden eyes that Ryker and his brothers had, her skin the same olive tone, and her hair the same caramel color.

"Oh, I like her, Ryker," she said with a chuckle. "Thank you, Francesca. That's very sweet."

"Okay, I'm heading out. Don't forget to dust tomorrow." She raised an eyebrow at her son. "I'll bring over Uncle Jack's brisket for you and Loch also. That man. He thinks Gable and Zeke are still here and makes way too much!" She looked at me. "It was very nice meeting you, Francesca."

"Nice meeting you too," I answered with a smile.

"Be good," she said to her son, tiptoeing up to kiss his cheek then got in her car and backed out of the drive and left.

I looked sheepishly at Ryker after she left. "Sorry."

He snorted. "Sorry?"

I shrugged. "Yeah, sorry."

"Get your gorgeous ass inside and I'll let you make it up to me." He swatted me on the butt making me yelp as I walked to the porch.

"You'll *let* me? Honey, you'll be *begging* me here pretty soon," I retorted.

"Oh, someone'll be begging, all right," he answered, putting his arm all the way around my neck to where my head was in the crook of it, and kissed the side of my head.

"Oh, God, please!" I begged Ryker.

He stood naked behind me and was trying to drive me insane.

When we'd gone inside after his mother left, we were all over each other, coats flying, lips locked, hands searching before finally making it to his bedroom because I'd reminded him that Loch could come home and I didn't want to be caught in flagrante.

Once in his room, he'd lain on the bed putting his hands behind his head, ankles crossed and ordered me to strip for him. I'd protested at first then thought, what the hell? I could tease the crap out of him in doing it. So I'd started by slowly taken my dress down one shoulder at a time, not showing him anything of significance for a while.

"Baby," he growled.

"What?" I asked all chastely, grinning at him seeing by the huge bulge in his pants what I was doing to him.

I turned my back to him, letting the dress drop lower in the front then the back to where he could see the top of my thong.

"Francesca," he warned.

I turned back to him with a smirk, covering my breasts as I let the dress drop to the floor and stood in front of him in only my thong, stockings and heels.

"Drop your arms."

"What?"

"You heard me," he said, all authoritatively which actually really turned me on.

"Oh, all right," I muttered letting one arm drop as I kept the other up still covering myself.

"That's it," he declared, getting up off the bed and stalking toward me like some dangerous jungle cat.

He took his tie off and grabbed me by my wrists putting them both in one hand and wrapping the tie around them.

"You're tying me up?" I screeched.

"Behave," he warned me yet again.

Then pulling me with him, he went to his closet, opening the door to pull out yet another tie. This one he put over my eyes, tying it behind my head.

"Wh-what're you doing?" I questioned, my hands clasped and my arms curled against my chest.

"Quiet," he whispered, taking my chin between his fingers then his mouth was on mine, not for a kiss but to suck on my bottom lip which was strangely erotic.

I heard him undressing and next the ripping of a condom, and then he was behind me as we were now, his hands coming around finding my nipples and rolling them between his thumbs and fingers as he pressed his erection against my bottom.

"Baby," I moaned when he put his palm against my belly and slowly slid his hand down to cup me between my legs, pushing his palm into me making me push my hips forward. Then his hand was gone.

I heard his knees crack as he knelt behind me and he smoothed his hands over the backs of my thighs down to my calves, back up to my bottom, squeezing each cheek before kissing each.

"Spread your legs for me," he demanded and I did as told.

He kissed the insides of each thigh just missing where I really wanted him, doing this several times, teasing, always teasing.

Not being able to see enhanced everything. His touch burned, his kisses pricked my skin, the teasing was tenfold frustrating.

"Ryker," I breathed out. "Please!"

I heard his dark chuckle again as he stood, smoothing his hands up my back then reaching them around to my front again, one drifting up to caress my breast, rolling my nipple, the other proceeding down where he slowly slid a finger through my folds, moving it to circle my clitoris lazily, then sliding his finger away and through my folds again then back to circle, over and over, all the while kissing my shoulder, his lips advancing up to kiss my neck then back beneath my ear before they traveled back down to the tendon between my neck and shoulder where he gave me a horse bite.

And that's where we were now, me begging him for more, him withholding, driving me crazy.

"Please, what?" he asked, sliding his cock between my legs back and forth, his breath hot against my neck.

"Please make love to me! Fuck me! Have me! Anything!" I cried out.

I felt him smile against my cheek. "That's my girl," he praised. His hand on my breast slid to my throat and gripped it, his fingers pressing in firmly holding my head against his chest. "You get to this point faster, Francesca, we can fuck faster. We clear?"

"Yes, God, yes!" I was dripping for him, could feel it running down my leg. "I need you, Ryker! Please!"

Keeping a hand on my throat, the other went behind me to grip his cock. He bent his knees and I felt him lining himself up then he slowly fed himself inside me. He retreated slowly and pushed back in slowly.

So slow.

Too slow.

"More!" I cried, literally cried because this was torture. "Please…" I choked out.

He finally gave me what I needed, thrusting up hard, impaling me, filling me over and over and I came harder than I ever had before. My body was electrified, every nerve ending lit up, on fire. I heard a scream so loud in the room, echoing off the walls, and realized it was my own. My God, what had he done to me?

Next, I found myself bent over the bed where he removed the ties from my eyes and wrists. He then turned me, picking me up and I wrapped my arms around his neck, my legs around his waist. Putting a knee to the bed, he crawled onto it, taking us to the center of it.

I felt him kiss my forehead. "You okay, baby?"

I pulled back, panting, to look at his beautiful face, and breathlessly nodded just as he thrust up inside me causing a loud moan that I had no control over to emerge from my throat. Now holding me close, his arms wrapped tightly around me, I knew he sensed that I was a bit out of it as he pumped his hips into me.

"You're mine, Francesca, understand?" he said huskily, his hips powerfully thrusting up again and again.

I nodded because I was his. Would always be his. He'd taken me higher than I'd ever been, and I loved it, loved him.

He came hard too, driving up so deep inside, his thrusts forceful, measured, and I held onto him tightly as he finished. He fell back on the bed me on top of him and we lay there in silence, our breathing the only sound in the room.

"I told you," he mumbled between breaths.

I had just enough energy to lift my head and look at him questioningly.

"Told you someone would be begging."

I nodded before dropping my head heavily onto his chest because he was not wrong.

We were in the kitchen having a midnight snack. We'd both passed out but I'd awakened just before midnight starving. I'd kissed him awake and told him to feed me. He was at the stove in a pair of gray shorts making grilled cheese sandwiches. I sat at the bar wearing the slate blue shirt he'd worn to dinner.

And we were having the talk. The one where he explained his rules and I was listening intently.

"I had two best friends growing up, Alex and Will. We did everything together." He flipped the sandwich and continued. "When we started middle school we all three signed up for wrestling. We were good. Alex was better than Will and me but that was okay. We were all in different weight divisions. In high school, we won the State Championship and all Alex and I were State Champs in our divisions. Will was a semi-finalist. But it was awesome. We all were getting recruited to wrestle in college."

He used the spatula to put the sandwich on a plate and brought it to me before going back to the stove to make his own. I ate as I listened.

"Alex was the best and was being recruited by the big dogs, the likes of Penn State and Minnesota. Will and I weren't as good so we'd planned on wrestling at Hallervan. Alex ended up going to Penn State and we were so proud. Our freshman year, when our schedules didn't conflict, Will and I would watch him either on TV or the school's website would stream it. He was doing so well. God, he was good."

He stopped to get more cheese out of the fridge and I remained silent as I finished my sandwich. I knew this was big for him and I knew letting him tell me with his back to me was the right thing to do too.

"He loved it. Penn State had won the national championship the year before and Alex contributed to their winning his freshman year. He was so excited about it. I'd never seen him so happy."

He flipped the sandwich and stared at the stove for a few minutes. I watched his broad back expand and contract as he took several deep breaths, the Grim Reaper looking even more heinous as if he himself were breathing. That made me shudder.

"Alex came home that summer for a couple weeks and all three of us got together to hang, chill whatever. One night Will called and said he and Alex were going to some all-night gym to workout. They wanted me to come with them but I had a girlfriend at the time and she didn't want me to go. Looking back, she was a controlling bitch and I should've cut her loose immediately."

Ah. The reason he never got serious with anyone since and also the reason he'd freaked out when I told him I loved him.

He put a sandwich on his plate and started making another one. He was quiet for so long I wasn't sure he'd continue.

"I tried calling them around one in the morning but neither answered. I went to bed thinking I'd talk to them in the morning."

More deep breaths.

"Got up the next morning and tried calling but still got no answer from either. I told my dad about it but he said they'd probably gotten drunk and were passed out."

He turned the sandwich.

"When I still hadn't heard from them by noon, I got really worried. I called Alex's house but no one answered there, so I called Will's."

He put the sandwich on the plate and turned off the burner keeping his back to me as he continued.

"Will's Aunt Lisa answered and she sounded like she was crying. That's when I knew something had happened."

Big breath.

I got up and went to him, hugging him from behind, just holding onto him.

"They'd gone to that stupid gym and worked out then went inside the steam room. Wrestlers do that sometimes to help them lose weight. Alex had been complaining that since he'd been home his mom's cooking was making him fat." He laughed. "He wrestled at 149 and had gained maybe ten pounds. It was no big deal."

He was quiet again and I rested my head against his back, holding on tight.

He blew out a breath. "They think the door to the steam room jammed and they couldn't get out. That or they'd passed out beforehand. They didn't find them until the next morning when someone went to clean it. The room was on a twenty-four hour timer so it went off at midnight, but a night worker reset it for them when they told him they wanted to go in."

He hung his head and I held on tight.

"Both of them gone in one shot. They were… they were like brothers to me. Such a waste." He turned around and wrapped me in his arms. "Such a fucking waste."

I kept my arms around him, resting my head on his chest listening to his heart pounding and realizing that's what the tattoo on his back was all about. Two dead warriors and one still fighting.

God.

"That's why I had to have rules. I needed to win for them. To fight for them. It's all been for them."

He gave me a squeeze.

"Then you came along and were a distraction and I didn't know how to make it work. I'd been so focused for so many years. That's all I knew was to stay focused. But I wanted you. God, how I wanted you. But I couldn't figure it out."

He leaned down and kissed the top of my head.

"Then you were gone and things got even worse. I kept telling myself I could go back to what I'd been doing that it'd been working. And I tried. But I couldn't get you out of my head." He pulled away and looked down at me. "You got in." He shook his head. "Somehow, you got in."

He bent to brush his lips against mine.

"You saved me, Francesca."

I looked up at him, my brow coming down.

He nodded as he said, "I knew it was all coming to an end and I didn't know what I'd do after. I mean, my brother went to the NFL. Basketball players can go to the NBA. Wrestlers can go pro and do that fake shit on TV or they can become MMA fighters. But then what? Only reason I'd do any of that would be for the money, not for Alex and Will. I've dedicated the last three years to my friends, my brothers, but I got lost this year not knowing where I was gonna go after. You saved me."

He picked me up and set me on the counter. "Like this shirt on you, baby," he said with a smirk. It was like a dress on me, hitting me mid-thigh. He put his hands on my thighs and pushed the shirt up, all the way to the bend of my legs at my hips. He saw that I didn't have on panties and looked up at me. "I really like this shirt on you."

I wrapped my arms around his neck and looked up at him. "I'm sorry for what happened. You've been a hero for your friends, wrestling in their honor. And you've done it well. So well. I'm proud to know you. I'm proud *of* you, Ryker. That's a lot for anybody to take on and you did it honorably. Do their families know?"

He shook his head.

"It doesn't matter. Alex and Will know what kind of man you are. Your family knows. I know. You're a good man, Ryker."

He stared at me for a long moment as if trying to find the right thing to say. And when he finally said it and it came out just fine.

"I love you, Francesca."

Ryker ended up not losing a match until he got to the National Championship where he eventually lost by one point in the semi-finals to the imminent champion.

The tournament was held in North Dakota and his family and I flew out to watch him. When he'd lost, I swear, I and everyone in his family had sucked in a breath, so worried about how he'd handle it.

But Ryker had gone to the winner and graciously shaken his hand then turned and looked up in the stands finding us and nodding as if to let us know he was okay.

Before he left the mat, he looked around for a moment knowing that would be his last time to ever be there. I teared up at that then started quietly crying watching as he then looked up to the ceiling where he raised his hand and pointed two fingers before leaving the floor.

Epilogue

When I was little, I used to be afraid of the dark. Yeah, so not proud of that now. Anyway, when I'd wake up and be scared, my mom would come in and sing the same song to me until I fell back to sleep. A line from the song always stuck with me, something about love not being love until you give it away.

I never knew what that line met until I met a more than beautiful, strong-willed, feisty woman who for some reason had decided I was her dream man. I still have to laugh at that but I'm so damned grateful that she picked me out of all the others out there.

Being with her has taught me that no matter how much you care about someone, if you're not willing to give them your heart, then it's all lights out, motherfucker, because that's not love at all.

Oh, I screwed around and almost lost her because I'd very fucking well done that at the beginning, being so full of myself thinking she should feel lucky that I was even giving her the time of day. When she turned the tables on me, well, that's when I got smart and did some serious thinking.

She tells me every day that she loves me and she's proud of me and all I can do is stare back at her in awe that she actually wants to be in my life. Seriously blows my fucking mind. I'm so not worthy of her it's ridiculous, but as long as she thinks I am, it works for me.

Looking back at how we ended up together, I think I may be able to pinpoint the exact moment I fell in love with her. I could say it was when she caught my dumbass making out with a girl who owned a pink VW Bug and she acted like she'd stopped by to have a look at it.

Or I could say it was when she was in her Treatment of Athletic Injuries class and I basically forced her to take me as her "patient" and she told me she hated me. That was pretty cute.

But no, in the end, I think the very moment I fell for her (I just didn't realize it at the time) was after I pretty much blackmailed her into going to O'Leary's with me after her class (man, I'm a dick). I'd pissed her off countless times over the course of the evening and she was getting ready to walk out on my sorry ass. And this next part right here, my friends, is the moment I fell hard for a brown-eyed Italian girl with the biggest heart of anyone I know.

She'd threatened to leave and I'd gotten up and blocked her in the booth not letting her get by. But that's not it. It's when I realized she be leaving and I didn't want her to go. I wanted her to be with me and it killed me to think she'd go and I might not get to see her again.

So yeah, the moment I fell was when I asked her to stay.

And she did.

Acknowledgments

To my lovely beta readers, Franca, Mel & Sam, I say it every time but you guys are too good to me. Thank you for all the last-minute stuff you take from me, and I mean ALL. You're the best ever! Your support means the world to me <3

To Stevie & the Hellbenders, you guys rock my world! Thank you for all the support and love you give me on the daily ;) You're the best! <3

Anne Mercier, I love you, woman! You always make time for me & I appreciate it so much, because I know you're either face first in your computer writing some sexy love scene or you're drooling over M. Shadows. Either way, thank you for always stepping away from the hotness for me!

TC Matson, Thank you for your friendship & never-ending support. I know I can come to you for the truth even though you think you'll upset me lol One of these days we're gonna do a Zak attack then die laughing at the little girl screams :P Lobe you!

Dawn Stanton, Thank you for pimping the hell out of my books. And while doing it, you, oh, you know, wrote a book lol You're amazing! Thank you for everything! You're a true friend & those are hard to find! #BeachHouse 2016 ;)

Amy Dunlap, Thank you for all you've done with the Hellbenders. Without you, that'd be the most boring place ever lol One of these days we'll hop on a plane, grab a hot cover model & knock back a few. Of course, you'll need to step over my trashed ass on your way out of the plane but know that my intentions were good (the road to hell & all, yeah, yeah) Love ya!

Erin Spencer, Thank you for always hooking me up at the last minute. I'm thinking you're starting to figure out my MO now so I'm past the shocking you stage. Thank you for being supportive with your sweet voice on my messenger :) Love you tons!

To the many bloggers who've spread the word about my books, thank you x a zillion. Know that you are appreciated GOBS!

And to the readers, this is all for you. Thank you <3

About the author:

USA Today Best Selling author Harper Bentley writes about hot alpha males who love hard. She's taught high school English for 23 years, and although she's managed to maintain her sanity regardless of her career choice, jumping into the world of publishing her own books goes to show that she might be closer to the ledge than was previously thought.

After traveling the nation in her younger years as a military brat, having lived in Alaska, Washington State and California, she now resides in Oklahoma with her teenage daughter, two dogs and one cat, happily writing stories that she hopes her readers will enjoy.

You can contact her at harperbentleywrites@gmail.com, at harperbentleywrites.com, on Facebook or on Twitter @HarperBentley